"You Should Come To Bed, Dharr," She Said.

Six feet two inches of potent prince, he faced Raina again. "There's only one bed on this plane and I would not wish to interrupt your sleep."

"Climb in, Dharr. You can be a good boy for one night."

"I could be very good, I assure you."

Before Raina could comment, he turned his back and snaked his pajamas down his hips.

She bolted upright. "What are you doing?"

"I prefer to sleep in the nude."

"So do I, but in deference to you, I've left my clothes on."

He snapped off the light, sending the cabin into total darkness. "Feel free to remedy that situation."

Dear Reader,

Welcome to another passionate month at Silhouette Desire where the menu is set with another fabulous title in our DYNASTIES: THE DANFORTHS series. Linda Conrad provides *The Laws of Passion* when Danforth heir Marc must clear his name or face the consequences. And here's a little something to whet your appetite—the second installment of Annette Broadrick's THE CRENSHAWS OF TEXAS. What's a man to do when he's *Caught in the Crossfire*— actually, when he's caught in bed with a senator's daughter? You'll have to wait and see....

Our mouthwatering MANTALK promotion continues with Maureen Child's *Lost in Sensation*. This story, entirely from the hero's point of view, will give you insight into a delectable male—what fun! Kristi Gold dishes up a tasty tidbit with *Daring the Dynamic Sheikh*, the concluding title in her series THE ROYAL WAGER. Rochelle Alers's series THE BLACKSTONES OF VIRGINIA is back with *Very Private Duty* and a hunk you can dig right into. And be sure to save room for the delightful treat that is Julie Hogan's *Business or Pleasure?*

Here's hoping that this month's Silhouette Desire selections will fulfill your craving for the best in sensual romance... and leave you hungry for more!

Happy devouring!

Melissa Jeglinski

Melissa Jeglinski
Senior Editor
Silhouette Desire

Please address questions and book requests to:
Silhouette Reader Service
U.S.: 3010 Walden Ave., P.O. Box 1325, Buffalo, NY 14269
Canadian: P.O. Box 609, Fort Erie, Ont. L2A 5X3

DARING THE DYNAMIC SHEIKH

KRISTI GOLD

Silhouette®

Desire

Published by Silhouette Books

America's Publisher of Contemporary Romance

SILHOUETTE BOOKS

ISBN 0-373-76612-2

DARING THE DYNAMIC SHEIKH

Visit Silhouette Books at www.eHarlequin.com

Printed in U.S.A.

Books by Kristi Gold

Silhouette Desire

Cowboy for Keeps #1308
Doctor for Keeps #1320
His Sheltering Arms #1350
Her Ardent Sheikh #1358
*Dr. Dangerous #1415
*Dr. Desirable #1421
*Dr. Destiny #1427
His E-Mail Order Wife #1454
The Sheikh's Bidding #1485
*Renegade Millionaire #1497
Marooned with a Millionaire #1517
Expecting the Sheikh's Baby #1531
Fit for a Sheikh #1576
Challenged by the Sheikh #1586
†Persuading the Playboy King #1600
†Unmasking the Maverick Prince #1606
†Daring the Dynamic Sheikh #1612

*Marrying an M.D.
†The Royal Wager

KRISTI GOLD

has always believed that love has remarkable healing powers and feels very fortunate to be able to weave stories of romance and commitment. As a bestselling author and a Romance Writers of America RITA® Award finalist, she's learned that although accolades are wonderful, the most cherished rewards come from personal stories shared by readers.

You can reach Kristi at KGOLDAUTHOR@aol.com, through her Web site at kristigold.com or by snail mail at P.O. Box 9070, Waco, Texas 76714. (Please include an SASE for a response.)

To Marilyn P., my favorite "Red Hat" lady,
talented writer and good friend.

Prologue

During his university career, Sheikh Dharr ibn Halim had learned the finer points of economics, yet he had mastered the art of seduction. He knew how to take a lover beyond the limit, how to use the cover of night to reveal a woman's secret passions and the light of day to heighten the pleasure. Yet over the past year, he'd learned all too well the devastation of love, a bitter lesson he would take with him the rest of his life.

Dharr was only mildly aware of the activities commencing outside the apartment he'd shared with two roommates during his Harvard career. He was in no mood to celebrate his accomplishments, for with his degree came the end to his time in America and the beginning of his responsibility to his country. Tomorrow he would be leaving everything behind, including his friends, Prince Marcel DeLoria, second born son of a European king and Mitchell Warner, a United States senator's son who knew all too well the burden of notoriety. Their time together had been a welcome distraction from the media's attention, a means for escape and an opportunity for revelations.

Dharr did not plan to make any disclosures during this farewell gathering. He chose to withhold the secret housed deep in his soul, never to be revealed to anyone. It was that secret that kept his thoughts occupied tonight as it had over endless nights in the recent past—he had fallen in love with a woman who had not loved him in return.

Seated in his favorite chair, Dharr turned his attention to his friends. As always, Mitch had positioned himself on the floor of their shared apartment as if he had an aversion to furniture. Marc had claimed his usual place on the sofa.

After a time, Mitch picked up the champagne bottle from the coffee table to refill each of their glasses. "We've already toasted our success," he said. "Now I propose we toast a lengthy bachelorhood."

Dharr leaned forward and raised his glass in agreement. "I would most definitely toast to that."

With champagne in hand, Marc paused a moment before offering, "I prefer to propose a wager."

Dharr and Mitch exchanged suspicious glances. "What kind of wager, DeLoria?" Mitch asked.

"Well, since we've all agreed that we're not suited for marriage in the immediate future, if ever, I suggest we hold ourselves to those terms by wagering that we'll all be unmarried on our tenth reunion."

Dharr knew he had a battle on his hands in showing his father the logic—and necessity—of waiting ten years to wed. He would endeavor to hold off at least that long, if he decided to marry at all. "And if we are not?"

"We will be forced to give away our most prized possession."

Mitch grimaced. "Give away my gelding? That would be tough."

Dharr could consider only one thing, the painting hanging above Mitch's head on the wall. That valuable piece was definitely his most cherished possession—now that the other had left him. "I suppose that would be my Modigliani original, and I must admit that giving away the nude would cause me great suffering."

"That is the point, gentlemen," Marc said. "The wager would mean nothing if the possessions were meaningless."

"Okay, DeLoria," Marc asked. "What's it going to be for you?"

"The Corvette."

"You'd give up the love mobile?" Mitch's tone resounded with the astonishment Dharr experienced over the offer. Marc coveted the blessed car as much as he coveted women.

"Of course not," Marc said. "I won't lose."

"Nor will I," Dharr said. "Ten years will be adequate before I am forced to produce an heir." And hopefully enough time to heal his wounds so that if he had to enter into a marriage, he would do so with honor, even if without love.

"No problem for me," Mitch said. "I'm going to avoid marriage at all costs."

Again Dharr held up his glass. "Then we are all agreed?"

Mitch touched his flute to Dharr's. "Agreed."

Marc did the same. "Let the wager begin."

Though Dharr would greatly miss the company of his friends, destiny dictated he accept his legacy and live up to his responsibilities. If the circumstances demanded he adhere to the marriage arrangement set out years before, at least he would have some satisfaction knowing that the young woman chosen for him had been born into his culture. She would understand his duty, his position, and what it would entail to be queen when the time came for Dharr to take over rule of his country, Azzril.

Should that prove to be the case, and if he could not have the woman he loved, then he would settle for Raina Kahlil, simply because she was the same as him.

One

Ten years later

She was nothing like he remembered.

Shading his eyes against the April afternoon sun, Dharr Halim realized the extent of Raina Kahlil's transformation from girl to woman as he covertly watched her from the deck of her California beachfront cottage. Several years had passed since those days when she'd possessed gangling limbs and unkempt braids. Today she was quite different, at least from a physical standpoint.

As she waded along the surf's edge, Raina moved with a grace as fluid as the ocean waves, her legs still long and lithe only with much more substance. Her gold-brown hair flowed over her shoulders like a cloak, trailing down her back where it touched the hollow of her spine below her waist. But it did not provide enough cover to completely conceal her golden flesh exposed by a two-piece swimsuit that left little to the imagination.

As far as Dharr could discern, she had yet to detect his presence, her gaze focused on a seashell she was examining as she headed toward him. Her distraction allowed more time to assess the unanticipated conversion.

She wore three silver loops in the lobe of each ear and a turquoise beaded necklace the color of her swimsuit. Her limited attire revealed the rise of her full breasts and her bare torso where Dharr's gaze tracked a path down her abdomen to her navel that sported a half-moon silver ring. Below that, the curve of her hips and thighs heightened his awareness of the drastic changes in her. And his awareness that as a man, he could appreciate those changes.

But the last time Dharr Halim had encountered his intended bride, she'd been in her early teens and engaged in hand-to-hand combat with a young boy who had dared to challenge her. Dharr wondered if she would attempt the same tactics when she discovered that he'd come to escort her back to Azzril.

Considering the way she carried herself—with unmistakable poise and confidence—Dharr suspected that her hellion attitude had undergone little alteration. When she sent him a look that might wither another man, he realized his assumption had been true. He had prepared himself for her reluctance, bolstered by information that should convince her to return home, despite the fact she had chosen to ignore his recent correspondence. He had not exactly prepared for the way his body reacted when he considered her fiery attitude might translate well beneath the cover of satin sheets, in the light of day or the dark of night. And that would be a fantasy he should resist. He had recently decided that he had no intention of upholding the marriage contract, cemented by the knowledge that she had rejected their culture. Out of respect for her and her father, he would maintain his distance even though he recognized he might be sorely tempted to do otherwise.

Without halting her progress, Raina strode up the stairs leading to the deck, assessing him much the same as he had her, yet she did not look happy over his unexpected presence. Somewhat surprised, yes, but definitely not pleased.

Stopping before him, she tossed the shell over one shoulder and braced both hands on her hips. "Well, as I live and breathe, if it's not the dashing Dharr Halim. Are you here to torment me like you used to?"

Her voice had lost all semblance of an Arabian accent, replaced by a distinct American tone, with a touch of sarcasm Dharr chose to ignore. He could not quite ignore her proximity or her body. "It is good to see you again, Raina."

"Answer my question. Why are you here?"

"Do I need a reason to visit?"

"As a matter of fact, yes, you do. It's been what? Fifteen years since we last met?"

"Twelve, to be exact. I was attending Harvard at that time and came home the summer before you left Azzril with your mother. Your father brought you to the palace for a visit. You were fighting with the cook's son."

"And you intervened, as usual." She hinted at a smile that quickly disappeared. "That was a long time ago, so don't you think I'm entitled to be a bit suspicious over your sudden appearance?"

"I promise my intentions are honorable." Even if his thoughts at the moment were not. A man would have to be struck blind— or a eunuch—not to have a reaction to her attire, the soft lines of her form that would feel quite exquisite against his hands.

She chafed her palms down her arms. "Let's continue this inside. It's kind of chilly out here."

She did not have to inform him of that fact, Dharr thought wryly when his gaze rested on her breasts. On the other hand, he was extremely warm.

Stepping to one side, he made a sweeping gesture toward the cottage. "After you."

"Good thing you didn't say 'ladies first.' I wouldn't have let you in."

As he'd suspected, she had not changed in regard to her independent spirit, but at least she had said it with a smile. "I would not presume to make such an error, Raina."

"Good." She glanced toward the drive where he'd parked the plain white sedan. "No limousine? No armed guards?"

"It's a rental car. Guards are not necessary at the moment." He smiled. "Unless you intend to throw me out."

"That depends on why you're here."

With that she passed by him, bringing with her the smell of sea and sun and a pleasing citrus scent. Once inside, she indicated a high-back stool at a bar that divided the small kitchen from the living area. "Have a seat. It's not much, but it's home."

Modest came to mind as he surveyed the area containing only a few pieces of furniture, followed by the awareness of light when she flipped two switches, completely illuminating the room and revealing a host of colors. Many different colors in varying hues, as if an artist's pallet had exploded, sending paint throughout the room. It suited her, Dharr decided, for she had always been a rather colorful character.

Dharr pulled back the stool and seated himself, expecting Raina to take the chair next to him. Instead she said, "I'm going to change and while I'm at it, you can tell me why you've come."

She swayed toward a bath diagonal to the counter and within his view, yet she left the door open, offering no protection or privacy from prying eyes—his eyes, in this instance. He could see the front of her torso in the vanity mirror she faced due to the open door. Although he thought it might be best to avert his eyes, he couldn't seem to force his gaze away from her body, admittedly intrigued that she would be so uninhibited.

When she reached for the ties around her neck, hidden beneath her hair, Dharr asked, "Do you not have a bedroom?" His voice held a noticeable edge, reflecting the sexual jolt he'd suffered when considering he might see more of her than he should.

The suit now unsecured, she anchored the top with one arm across her breasts. "You're looking at it."

Yes, he was, and he liked what he saw when she lowered the top—teardrop breasts tipped with russet nipples that would fit perfectly in his hands and mouth. The house, however, did not interest him. He scooted the stool beneath the counter to hide his reaction to her.

"Now tell me to what do I owe this visit?" she said as she slipped the bottoms down. Dharr could only make out faint details of her well-shaped buttocks due to the vanity concealing the reflection from her waist up and her hair, which covered most of her back. Yet it was enough to leave him nearly bankrupt of all thought.

He cleared his throat. "Had you read my letters, then you would know why I have come."

"What letters?" She slipped a silky coral shirt over her head and Dharr watched the fabric slide down, imagining his own hand doing the same over her hair, or her bare back. Only he would keep going, lower and lower…

"Dharr, what letters?" she asked as she pulled her hair from beneath the shirt and tugged on a pair of underwear made of sheer lace. Black lace, and barely enough fabric to be considered an article of clothing.

He shifted on the stool once more. "I've recently sent two letters. Did you not receive them?"

Finally she worked a pair of loose-fitting slacks up her hips, turned and came back into the room. "I didn't get any letters. Did you send them here?"

"I had my assistant send them. Perhaps they went to the wrong address."

She pulled her hair up and secured it with a black band high atop her head. "I've just recently moved from my mother's house. Maybe she has them."

"Perhaps she does."

She leaned over the counter and scrutinized him with golden eyes as clear as a fine gemstone. "I could call her and ask, but since you're here, why don't you just tell me in your own words what they said?"

The news that Dharr had to deliver would not be pleasant, therefore he would work his way into it. He rose from the stool and walked past her into the small living area, stopping to view a canvas resting on an easel near the large paned window facing the driveway. The painting was of a young girl turned profile, standing in the midst of a desert, looking out over mountainous terrain. The child appeared small and lost among the expanse of sand.

He glanced at Raina now leaning back against the counter. "Did you do this?"

"Yes, I did. It's a memory I had of Azzril when I was a little girl. I remember feeling very insignificant in all that open space."

"It's very good," he said, then strolled back to the counter and reclaimed his place across from her. "Do you support yourself with your art?"

She crossed her arms and propped them on the counter. "No. I teach at a small private college. I have a master's in art history. And you still haven't answered my question. What did your letters say, and what are you doing here?"

"I am here at the request of your father."

Her eyes narrowed, flashing anger. "This better not have anything to do with that archaic marriage arrangement."

"I assure you it does not. As far as I am concerned, that no longer exists."

She rolled her eyes to the ceiling. "Try telling that to my father. I'm sure he'll have something to say about it."

"You will have to take that up with him when you see him in the next few days."

She straightened. "Papa's coming here?"

"No. Your father wishes you to come to Azzril immediately. He sent me to escort you back."

She sighed. "Dharr, I'm an adult, not a child. I don't just up and leave when my father says so, I don't care what he wishes."

"What if it is your father's final wish?"

"I don't understand." Raina sounded unsure and looked almost as forlorn as the child in the painting.

Dharr had hated saying something that he did not exactly believe to be the truth, but Idris Kahlil had insisted Dharr present a dire situation to convince Raina to come to Azzril. Yes, the former sultan did have a potentially serious illness, yet suggesting he was pounding on death's door was somewhat an exaggeration.

"Your father quite possibly has a heart condition, Raina. He has been restricted to bed rest at this time."

Her face was shrouded in disbelief. "He was just here to see me two months ago."

The revelation took Dharr aback. As far as he'd known, the sultan had not been in contact with his daughter beyond phone calls. "He has been here?"

"Yes. Every year, sometimes twice a year, since I left Azzril. The last time I saw him, he looked fine."

"He's not a young man, Raina."

"But he's so strong. I can't believe…"

Dharr thought he detected tears before she lowered her eyes. He felt compelled to provide comfort and took her hand into his, somewhat surprised when she failed to pull away. Her long, delicate fingers seemed fragile in the well of his palm and he experienced a surge of protectiveness toward her, as he had many years before. "You are his only child, Raina. His only family. He needs you to be with him during his recovery."

She raised her gaze to his, optimism replacing the distress on her beautiful face. "Then he's going to recover?"

Undoubtedly he would, Dharr thought. The sultan was not a man to let illness restrain him for long. "The physicians are not certain about the extent of his condition at this time, but he's in no imminent danger. They are being cautious and watching him closely. He has been resting comfortably since his departure from the hospital."

She pulled her hands from his grasp, leaving Dharr feeling strangely bereft. "He's not in the hospital?"

"He was. For a day after he suffered the chest pains. Though they advised against it, he insisted he did not need their care."

"He's so damn stubborn," Raina muttered.

Dharr recognized that Raina was very much her father's daughter. "Yes, and it would help greatly if you could convince him to rest."

Her laugh was without mirth. "Short of chaining him to the bed, I doubt I could keep him there if he doesn't want to cooperate."

"I am hoping you can persuade him."

She stared at some focal point above Dharr's head for a few moments before saying, "School doesn't end until next month. I'd have to find someone to take my classes."

"Is that possible?"

Raina seemed to be running on automatic, her eyes unfocused, most likely from the unanticipated news. "Yes. And I would need to pack, of course. I should probably call Mother, but I can do that when I arrive in Azzril. Otherwise, she might try to talk me out of going."

"Then I assume you have decided to come with me?"

She frowned at him. "What choice do I have? If Papa needs me, then I have to be there for him."

Dharr was pleased—and surprised—she had not presented any real resistance. "We can leave in the morning. I have my private jet awaiting instructions for our return."

"I want to leave tonight."

Another unexpected revelation. "Would it not be best if you had a decent night's sleep?"

"It's a twenty-hour flight. I can sleep on the plane."

"If that is what you wish."

"It is." She pushed away from the counter. "I'll take a quick shower and then make a call to the school's headmaster. If you want something to drink, you'll find it in the fridge."

He greatly wanted to join her in the shower, another unwise idea. She rushed into the bathroom, this time closing the door, leaving Dharr alone to make his own calls from the cellular phone. After he'd arranged for the flight to leave tonight, he took the opportunity to look around while Raina prepared for the trip. She had several other oils on display aside from the one of the girl, but the painting set on an easel in the corner drew his attention. Although it was not complete, he had no trouble discerning it was a partially nude woman with long light brown hair staring out to sea, a man standing next to her, his face turned into her temple, one arm laid across her back and his hand resting at the top of her buttocks in a show of possession.

Dharr experienced an unexpected stab of jealousy that perhaps this man was Raina's lover. Perhaps they had stood near this very place, taking in the view after having made love. But he would not confront her with his suspicions. He'd had no reason to expect her to remain celibate. She had been free to do as she pleased with whomever she pleased. She still was.

Even though he had no plans to have Raina Kahlil as his wife, he could still imagine what it might be like to have her in his bed.

And those fantasies should remain as such—only fantasies. Yet he was about to embark on a twenty-hour journey with a woman who had undeniably captured his interest. A true test of his fortitude. He would not succumb to baser urges, even though one definite part of his anatomy might be telling him otherwise.

It was absolutely huge.

Raina had been expecting some kind of a smaller private jet, not an enormous hunk of flying metal with a 7 in its identifying number. But why was she so surprised? Dharr Halim wouldn't settle for halfway in his chosen mode of transportation or anything else he endeavored.

Still, she hated flying with a passion. In fact, she hadn't flown since the night she'd left Azzril for America. If it hadn't been for her father's illness, she would never have stepped on a plane again. But she did step onto this plane, immediately greeted by a steward dressed in a tuxedo. "Welcome, Miss Kahlil and Sheikh Halim. I will be available to tend to your needs."

Not exactly in the mood to be overly polite, Raina sent him a smile and a muttered, "Thanks."

"We will contact you when we are ready for dinner," Dharr said from behind her.

As Raina walked the plane's aisle, Dharr followed at a minimal distance, making her more nervous with every step they took. He'd always made her nervous, even when she'd been a girl—the kind of discomfort that stemmed from being in the presence of a man too magnetic for his own good. Too gorgeous to ignore with his unreadable dark eyes and a body that would make many a woman fall at his feet and kiss the expensive loafers he walked in. And in part, because she'd known from the time she was a child that he'd been chosen for her. She'd recognized his charisma long before she'd admitted to liking boys of any kind. But she'd been quick to deny she'd had a minor crush on him, even if she had.

But she couldn't allow any attraction to him at all. They were too, too different. Her mother and father had never worked through those differences, and their estrangement had almost destroyed Raina. She loved them both to excess, but she'd grown up as a pawn in their war of wills—until recently. Now she was on her own and she would make her own decisions. That did not include bending to her father's insistence that she marry Dharr Halim, in accordance with tradition. She had no desire to do anything with Dharr Halim.

Okay, that wasn't exactly true. The minute she'd discovered him standing on her deck, looking imposing and as breathtakingly handsome as he had the last time she'd seen him, she'd imagined doing a few things with him that didn't involve matrimony. More like consummation.

Two men in dark suits stood as she passed by an area that looked like a lounge with eight white seats, two facing two others on her left, the same on her right, televisions suspended above each group of chairs.

The men—bodyguards she presumed—offered her courteous smiles and nodded at Dharr as he moved around her and told them in Arabic, "We are not to be disturbed."

Raina was disturbed. Very disturbed. She didn't like the thought of being hidden away with a man whose every move showcased his sensuality, his power. But she followed him anyway when he glanced over his shoulder and said, "This way."

He paused to shrug off his coat and tossed it on one row of seats but left the white kaffiyeh, secured by the ornate gold and blue band indicating his royal status—the one thing that differentiated him from the rest of the occupants on the plane, setting him apart from most men Raina had known, aside from her father. It served as a symbol of prestige, wealth and all the things Raina had cast off since she'd gone to America as a teenager. She preferred keeping company with surfers and recreational sailors, common folk, not crowns or kaffiyehs.

Yet she couldn't help but notice the way Dharr's black slacks adhered to his really nice butt, the expanse of his wide shoulders and the breadth of his back covered in a white tailored dress shirt, the way he moved with a hint of cockiness as if he expected everyone to bow and scrape in his presence. Raina didn't do bowing or scraping or drooling even though her mouth was oddly starting to water.

Obviously she was hungry. That was it. She hadn't had dinner.

Dharr led her past a few other groupings of chairs and a spiral staircase. As they ascended, she grasped the rail tightly so she wouldn't slip and fall since she continued to secretly regard his rear-end. When they reached the top, he opened a door to reveal…a bed? A queen-size bed covered by an ivory satin spread, built-in cabinets positioned on either side of the bulkhead. A regular recreational vehicle with wings.

Raina stopped and stared at Dharr who was now facing her. "That's a bedroom." And that was a brilliant observation.

His half smile showed a glimpse of perfect white teeth.

"Yes, it has a bed, but it also has a sitting area and serves as my office. We will be afforded more privacy here."

More privacy was a problem, Raina decided. She didn't think she should get anywhere near a bed with Dynamic Dharr in the room, especially behind a closed door in a plane with no way out aside from an emergency exit. She refused to sit up all night with a bunch of bodyguards or ride on the wing for the majority of the trip if he got out of hand.

She was being silly. Dharr hadn't made any overtures other than taking her hand, and that had been a comforting gesture. He certainly hadn't indicated that he wanted to get her into bed. And why was that whole concept of getting into bed with him making her shaky and sweaty all at the same time?

That didn't matter. She could do this. She could go into Dharr Halim's traveling bedroom and keep her distance.

When she failed to move, he asked, "Are you coming?" in a low, dangerous voice. The image of him saying the same thing to her in the throes of passion vaulted into her brain and took away her breath.

She shifted the yellow nylon bag from one shoulder to the other, the bag Dharr had insisted on carrying but she hadn't let him. Right now it felt as if it were weighted with bricks, not the few things she'd thrown together for her brief stay.

She encouraged her feet to move forward, move toward the room, and once inside, she was relieved to find that to her left, a table and more seats did exist, along with a built-in desk.

After dropping her bag on the floor and nudging it beneath the edge of the bed with one foot, she perched on the mattress and tested it with a push of her palm. "This is comfy."

"Yes, it is. Very accommodating."

She looked up to see Dharr's eyes had turned jet-black, sending her off the mattress as if she'd been shot out of a rocket launcher.

He indicated the two side-by-side chairs opposite the bed. "We will need to be seated here for take-off. After the pilot gives the clearance, you will be free to do as you wish, and sit—or lie down—wherever you wish."

Sitting seemed to be the smartest thing to do.

On that thought, Raina occupied the seat away from the window. She despised take-offs and landings the most. Her father had recognized her fear of flying, the reason why he'd come to California instead of expecting her to make the long trip to Azzril. But tonight, she would have to face her fears in order to make sure her papa's illness wasn't serious. As frustrating as he could be at times, as unbendable, she would die if anything happened to him.

Dharr settled into the seat beside her without giving her a second glance. He smelled great, like a forest after a rain, clean and fresh and full of secrets to behold.

She stared at him for a moment, wondering if his hair was still as thick and dark as it had been all those years ago. "Is that necessary, your kaffiyeh?"

He looked insulted. "In business, yes. It commands respect."

"But you're not on business now."

"True." He raked the covering from his head and tossed it onto the table not far away, confirming that his hair was still as gorgeous. Then he turned his deadly grin on her. "Is there anything else you wish me to remove?"

Her skin threatened to slink off her body with the pleasant thought of him taking everything off. "Very funny."

"I'm glad I have amused you."

He wasn't amusing her at all. In fact, he was making her perspire even more with his toxic smile and his bedtime black eyes.

A voice came over the intercom announcing they'd been cleared for take-off, shattering the moment and startling Raina.

Dharr sent her a look of concern as he fastened his seat belt. "Are you afraid of flying, Raina?"

She didn't dare admit she was afraid of anything, even if she was. She stared straight ahead so he couldn't see that fear when the plane began to back away from the gate. "I'm not fond of planes. Obviously—"

"Raina—"

"...they were designed by men, if you consider their shape."

"Raina—"

"Giant phallic symbols with massive engines."

"Raina."

She shot a glance at Dharr. "What?"

"Fasten your seat belt."

Great. The only thing protecting her from getting tossed around like rag doll and she'd almost forgotten to put it on.

After she snapped her belt and secured it, she sat back and gripped the arms of the seat. The plane taxied toward the runway while Raina did her best to think positive thoughts, to no avail. She loathed feeling so out of control.

"I think I should cut holes in the floor and run to help this thing get off the ground," she muttered. "It's unnatural, expecting something so big to take you airborne."

Dharr leaned over, his warm breath wafting across her cheek. "Some say that size can be important when it comes to achieving greater heights."

She gave him a mock-serious look. "You haven't changed a bit, Dharr Halim. Always the tease. But it seems you've graduated from tormenting me about my bony knees to delivering questionable innuendo."

He raked a slow glance down her body. "And you have graduated from the bony stage. If you recall, you were the one who compared the plane to a phallic symbol. I was simply following your lead."

Before Raina could deliver a retort, the engines whined to life. She closed her eyes, bracing for the moment when the tube of steel raced down the narrow strip of asphalt and hurled them into the air, hopefully without incident.

The louder the engine roared and the faster the plane went, the harder Raina gripped the arm of the seat. "Come on, come on, come—"

Dharr's mouth covered hers, cutting off her nervous chant and her random thoughts of doom. Raina didn't remember this being a part of the in-flight safety instructions. Didn't remember ever getting this kind of service—service with a capital S. In fact, she didn't even remember her name.

He introduced his tongue slowly, concisely, in a feather-soft incursion between her parted lips. She felt light-headed, breathless, when he pulled her left hand out of its death grip on the seat's arm and twined his fingers with hers. She melted more and more into mindlessness with every foray of his sinful tongue. Her heart rate started climbing and climbing with the plane, but she wasn't concerned with the plane. She wasn't concerned about anything as the kiss continued, growing deeper, more insistent with each passing moment. She only cared about Dharr's mouth moving gently against hers. His scent, his taste, his skill.

Dharr finally pulled away and sent her another heat-inducing smile. "I believe we have successfully completed the take-off."

Raina leaned over to look out the window, seeing nothing but sky, the setting sun and wisps of clouds. She had no idea how long the kiss had lasted or why she'd even allowed it. And she was fighting mad that Dharr had taken advantage of her fear. "Why did you do that?"

"To bring your mind and body to another plane aside from this one."

She had to admit, he'd done that, and quite sufficiently. "That wasn't playing fair."

"I was not playing, Raina. I was very serious." If his expression was any indication, he was dead serious. Seriously seductive.

"I guess I should thank you," she murmured.

"You are welcome. And should you wish me to divert your attention again during our flight, please inform me."

Of all the shifty sheikhs. "Well, thanks so much for asking my permission this time."

He raised a dark brow. "This time?"

She sent him a sharp look. "The last time. We are not going to do this."

"I believe we already have." He touched her face and slid one finger over her cheek, slowly, methodically, hypnotically. "Anything else you require of me, you need only ask."

She required only one thing, his absence so she could keep a tight grip on her control. But since it didn't look as if he were going anywhere for the next twenty hours, she realized she would have to be strong. Otherwise, she might end up using that nearby bed for something other than sleeping.

No way, Jose. She would be damned if Dharr Halim, with all his blatant self-assurance and magnetic machismo, would be her ticket to the Mile-High Club.

Two

Raina Kahlil would make an excellent lover. Dharr had decided that the moment he'd spontaneously kissed her. A rather good beginning to their reintroduction—and a dangerous one at that. However, he had not been able to think of any other means to allay her fears, or so he'd tried to convince himself. Yet he had been successful with his distraction. He had also awakened his own libido, which would result in a long, hard journey back to Azzril.

Raina also put everything into eating, as well, he realized, as she consumed the cold vegetable sandwich without bothering to look up. Odd that she'd grown so silent since they'd become airborne. He never remembered her being prone to keeping her thoughts to herself, even when she had been a young girl. Especially then.

She pushed aside her empty plate and dabbed at her face with a napkin, drawing Dharr's attention to her full lips. "That was wonderful."

"I apologize for not having a hot meal, but we had little time to prepare."

"The sandwich was great."

He picked up the bottle of Bordeaux from the table and held it aloft. "Would you like more wine?"

"Considering the altitude, I'd probably get drunk if I had another."

He refilled her glass then set the bottle aside. "Perhaps you would relax if you had another."

"I *am* relaxed." She pushed the glass away, knocking it off balance.

Dharr grabbed it up before it tipped over, saving the beige carpet from scarlet stains. He could not save his smile from making an appearance. "Are you certain?"

"Yes. I'm just clumsy." She folded her hands before her on the table. "So tell me, Dharr, are you completely in control these days?"

"In control of what?" Certainly not of his carnal urges in her company.

"Are you running the country?"

General conversation. He would participate for the time being, as long as she didn't ask too many personal questions. "My parents are traveling now and I have taken over most of my father's duties, although he is still king."

"Has Azzril changed much?"

"We have expanded the university in Tomar as well as the hospital. We are developing more modern agricultural methods and aiding the poorer towns with their growth."

"Do you have any women?" He could tell she regretted the query when her gaze wandered away. "I meant any women in power."

Dharr sat back with wineglass in hand, greatly enjoying the

slight rise of color on cheeks. He wondered how she would look flushed all over. "Yes, doctors, legal representative, professors."

She finally brought her golden eyes back to his. "What about government positions?"

The positions he was currently pondering had nothing to do with politics. "Not presently, but it is only a matter of time. Are you interested?"

"Heck, no. I was just curious. My mother always complained that women had little power in Azzril."

At one time, that had been true. But Dharr had made great strides over the past ten years. "And your mother, is she well?"

Raina picked up the napkin, kneading it much like the family cook had kneaded the evening bread when he'd been a boy. "My mother's lonely. She's never dated anyone since she left Papa."

"As I understand it, she is still married to your father."

Raina twisted the napkin with a vengeance. "Technically, yes. Neither of them has even considered divorce. I think that's ridiculous. If they aren't going to live together, why not just end it so they can move on with their lives?"

Dharr noted a flash of pain in her eyes and knew that her parents' estrangement had not been easy on her. "Perhaps they are both too full of pride. And divorce is still frowned upon in Azzril."

"My mother's from America where divorce is as commonplace as cars on the Los Angeles freeways."

He rested his hand on hers when she released her death grip on the napkin. "And commitment is taken too lightly."

She pulled her hand from beneath his and shrugged. "If you can't live together peacefully, why prolong the agony?"

"I suppose in some ways you are right, but I see marriage as an agreement that can be mutually beneficial if kept in proper perspective."

"What benefit would that be?"

He took a drink of his wine then leveled his gaze on her. "I can think of many ways a man and woman can benefit from each other. Procreation, for one. The process of procreating is another."

She folded her arms beneath her breasts, looking defiant. "All the great sex and babies in the world can't help a bad relationship. Passion fades and if there's nothing left after that, then all you have is a piece of paper and hatred."

"If you do not give yourself over to emotions, then hate would not enter into it. Respect is more important."

"Then you're saying that love should be avoided at all costs?"

"Are you saying that you believe in something as frivolous as love?"

"I've never been in love with a man, but my love for my parents is very real. Don't you love yours?"

"Yes, but that is different."

"How so?"

"I know that my parents' love for me is without conditions."

Her smile was wan. "Oh, I see. Someone has broken your heart."

How could she know that? Was he being too transparent? "I simply do not feel that it's wise to give yourself over to intangible emotions."

Raina stood, her golden gaze fixed on his. "Being such a cynic must be very tiresome."

"Where are you going?" he asked as she moved from behind the table.

"To the little girls' room, then I'm going to get ready for bed, if that's okay with you, Sheikh Halim."

"I have no objection. That is why the bed has been provided."

She smiled a skeptic's smile. "Oh, I just bet you put that bed in here for sleeping."

"Why else?"

"Don't play dumb with me, Dharr. I know you've had women on this flying love machine before. A man like you wouldn't spend his adult life without a few lovers."

That he could not deny, but there had not been all that many, and none had been more than a means for gratification. Except one. "Have you, Raina?"

She pulled her bag from beneath the bed and slipped the strap over her shoulder. "Have I what?"

"Taken lovers?"

"That's none of your business." With a determined lift of her chin, she turned away and disappeared into the bathroom. He had to agree, it was not his concern. That did not prevent him from wondering if her defensiveness resulted from the fact she had taken several lovers, or perhaps none. He preferred to believe the latter, although he could not explain why. Could not explain the envy when considering another man had touched her. Perhaps he was only being protective, or a fool.

A few minutes later, she came out of the small bath wearing a sleeveless royal blue satin shift that barely touched the top of her thighs. Dharr swiveled the anchored chair away from the table to face her as she turned her back to him. He watched while she bent over to replace her bag beneath the bed, revealing sheer white panties, not lace this time, but still impacting Dharr's desire for her. She pulled back the covers, fluffed her pillow, stretched out on her back and pulled the sheet up to her waist.

"Are you coming to bed anytime soon?" she asked, failing to look at him.

"I did not know you were interested in having me in your bed."

She raised her head and scowled. "To sleep, Dharr. This bed is big enough for both of us. You stay on your side, I'll stay on mine, and we'll be fine and dandy."

Dharr leaned back in the chair and assessed her with a long glance over her body concealed by the sheet. "I assure you it would be most difficult for me to remain on my side of the bed, unless you erect a wall between us." Dharr was fighting a different kind of erection at the mere thought of lying next to her and eventually on top of her.

"Oh, so you're not strong enough to just sleep with a woman without *sleeping* with a woman?"

"Quite possibly I could with certain women, but not a woman such as yourself, especially since you are wearing very little clothing."

She lifted the sheet and peeked beneath it as if she had no memory of what she wore. "I'm adequately covered."

After dropping the sheet, she rolled to her side and faced him, her cheek resting on her arm partially tucked beneath the pillow. "If I were at home, I wouldn't have anything on. I don't like wearing clothes to bed."

Dharr experienced a definite rise in temperature and a rise below his belt. Yet he didn't bother hiding his current state of arousal by crossing his legs. In fact, he stretched his legs before him so she would know what she was doing to him. At least then he could say he'd given her substantial warning, even if not a verbal one. "I certainly understand, Raina. I do not favor clothes at bedtime either. If that makes you uncomfortable, I will stay in this chair."

She sent a direct look at his lap, then said, "Fine. Good night."

That was not what Dharr wanted at all. He'd wanted her to be more persistent, had hoped she would encourage him to join her. But her eyes drifted closed and it wasn't long before her face relaxed with sleep.

However, he was not relaxed nor would he be when plagued with the fantasy of stripping out of his clothing and crawling in beside her, waking her with the most intimate of kisses, with touches that would make her body beg for his consideration. He could give her pleasure, but he would have to be satisfied to leave it at that. And that would not be acceptable. Not unless he considered her as the woman who would remain at his side as future queen.

At Harvard, he'd thought he had found the woman he wanted to make his wife, only to learn that she could never accept his legacy or his culture. She had led him on a sensual adventure then closed the door on any future they might have had together, walking away without even a personal goodbye, only a letter that told him they could never be together permanently.

And he would have given everything up for her. Everything. Even his heart. Never again.

Raina slowly returned to consciousness after drifting in and out of fitful sleep. Disoriented, she thought she was back in her childhood bed in Azzril, until she looked to her left and saw the rectangular windows revealing night sky and heard the hum of jet engines. Then she remembered. She wasn't fourteen; she was twenty-five. She was on a plane bound for a country that was only a distant memory, and the euphoria she'd experienced only moments before had been the result of a dream.

A dream involving her mother and father holding her hand as she walked between them in the streets of Tomar, suspended in a time before her mother had stolen away in the night to board a plane bound for the U.S., taking her daughter on a journey full of turbulent weather and equally turbulent emotions.

Raina's world had come apart on that dreadful flight, and she'd experienced real fear for the first time in her life, not only from the horrible trip but also from a total loss of security knowing she would be entering a strange land without her beloved father. Worse, she hadn't even told her papa goodbye.

"I see you have awakened."

She turned her face toward the deep, controlled voice that floated over her like a satin veil against sensitive skin. Light from the lamp attached to the desk spilled over him, providing more than adequate illumination for Raina to get the full effect of the picture he now presented. If she had paints and a canvas, she would immortalize him—a portrait of dark against light. A representation of overt sexuality and undeniable power.

He looked as proud and regal as if seated on a throne instead of a chair. As dangerous as if he were a thief of hearts assessing his next victim with eyes as black as a bottomless cavern. His soft, sensuous lips, surrounded by a shading of whiskers, contrasted with the sharp, angular lines of his cheeks, his solid jaw and the straight plane of his nose.

His arms rested on the chair's arms in casual indifference, his large hands curled over the ends, the right one sporting a gold and ruby signet ring on his little finger. His well-defined biceps conveyed his physical strength; his forearms laced with prominent veins and a fine covering of dark hair revealed his absolute maleness. As did his bare chest where a spattering of crisp, dark hair covered his pectorals and surrounded his pale brown nipples before tapering into a V pointing downward toward his ridged abdomen.

Raina visually followed the strip of hair below his navel to the waistband of the pajamas he now wore. But she didn't stop there though she recognized she should. Instead she homed in on the dark shading at his groin apparent through the thin, white muslin material.

She knew she should quit looking, knew that her curiosity could get her into trouble if she didn't. But she couldn't tear her eyes away from the prominent crest that indicated he was aroused. Very aroused. And so was Raina when she imagined holding intimate knowledge of that very male part of him in her hands, deep inside her body.

She finally forced her gaze back to the ceiling and kicked off the covers, bending her knees, causing her nightshirt to slide to the tops of her thighs. Before she'd seen him sitting there, watching her, she'd been comfortable, even chilly. But now… Now she was incredibly hot, from the crown of her head to the tips of her toes.

She heard the chair creak but didn't dare look at him, not after she'd shamelessly appraised him like a jeweler's patron searching for the perfect diamond. He was as fine and flawless as a twenty-carat stone featured front and center in the display case. Raina wished he were behind glass now so she wouldn't be so tempted to further examine him, or to touch him.

"How long have I been out?" she asked, her voice husky from sleep and a desire for him that made little sense.

"No more than two hours." His voice was no less deep, no less lethal.

She afforded him a quick glance. "Two hours? That's all?"

"Yes. Did you not find the bed to your liking?"

"It's very comfortable." Raina wasn't, not in the least. "It's kind of warm in here, though."

"Do you wish me to turn up the air?"

"That would be great." Although she doubted any amount of air would relieve the heat coursing through her body.

He rose from the chair and walked to the bed, reaching up to adjust the round vents above her head. Just seeing the tuft of dark hair underneath his arm made her shiver.

He stared down on her, his gaze roaming over her bare thighs covered in goose bumps before coming to rest on her satin-covered breasts that tightened from his perusal. "Are you too cold now?"

"No."

"Are there any more adjustments you wish me to make?"

He dropped his hand from the vents and brushed his knuckles over his groin, as if inviting her to do the same. With little effort, she could touch him there. Linger there to learn if he was as powerful as he looked. Clamping her knees closed in response to the damp wash of heat between her thighs, she turned her attention back to the ceiling and gave herself a good mental chastising.

Her reaction to him was outrageous. She didn't really know him. She wasn't even sure she still liked him. But she was only human—all too human—and this physical attraction, this chemistry, if left unabated could cause her a world of problems.

"I'm fine now," she said, although she didn't sound at all fine.

"Good. Please let me know if I can assist you further."

Oh, he could, in some terribly wicked ways. She needed to stop thinking about that, stop fantasizing about him. After all, she only had fifteen or so hours to go in his company. She could manage that without turning into some sex-crazed female need factory.

What a crock, she thought when she blurted, "You should come to bed," after he turned around to return to the chair.

He faced her again, looking provocative with the lamp's glow as a backdrop. Six feet two inches of potent prince. Darkness and light. "I would not wish to interrupt your sleep."

"And I don't want to be blamed when you can't walk tomorrow because you're too stiff." Raina wanted to bite her tongue off the minute the words left her mouth.

His eyes narrowed and his smile made another slow, sultry appearance. "You are very observant, Raina."

She rolled her eyes, affecting disgust, when in reality her

whole body felt as if he'd lit a match to it. "I meant stiff as in a sore neck." She scooted over, practically hugging the wall, and patted the pillow beside her. "Climb in, Dharr. You can be a good boy for one night."

"I could be very good, I assure you."

Realizing she was playing a perilous game of chance, Raina almost rescinded the offer. But before she could, Dharr turned his back and snaked his pajamas down his hips, revealing his bare bottom and the backs of his hair-covered thighs.

She bolted upright like a jack-in-the-box. "What are you doing?"

He regarded her over one shoulder as he crossed the area, his muscled buttocks flexing with each step he took toward the desk. "I've told you, I prefer to sleep in the nude."

"So do I, but in deference to you, I've left my clothes on."

He snapped off the light, sending the cabin into total darkness. "Feel free to remedy that situation. I will not see anything this time."

"What do you mean 'this time'?"

She could hear the floor rasp as he approached the bed, sensed his presence even before he spoke again. "At your house earlier, you left the bathroom door open while you changed."

"That was so I could hear you."

"Are you certain it was not so that I could see you? Because I did see you, Raina. In the open door. In the mirror's reflection. And I have suffered the effects all evening."

Actually she'd assumed that from his position at the bar he hadn't been able to see anything, and she hadn't considered anything beyond his sudden appearance. Yet the thought of him watching her undress brought back the utter need, the searing heat.

The mattress bent with his weight and although it was basically pitch dark, the limited light coming from the windows allowed her to make out his profile as he stretched out on his back, his hands laced behind his neck.

If she knew what was good for her, Raina would lower the flaps over the windows so she couldn't see any details. She would turn over and smash her mouth against the wall to keep from answering the urge to kiss him. Before she asked him to make good on his promise to be very good.

Instead she fell back against the bed, as inflexible as a steel beam, her hands rigid at her sides. No way on earth could she go to sleep like this. She flipped over onto her stomach and buried her face in the pillow, her gown now scrunched up beneath her belly. This was why she didn't wear anything to bed. She hated having to tug and pull and adjust fabric that had managed to knot beneath her or practically crawl up around her neck.

She considered taking off the nightgown. Why not? Dharr hadn't thought twice about removing his pajamas, and he had suggested she do that very thing. Besides, he couldn't see her, and she could leave her panties on. He hadn't moved so he could already be asleep. Still, that meant both of them would wake in the morning in bed together, without clothes and with only a few inches separating them. He might get the wrong idea. Or was it the right idea?

No. She couldn't allow him to make love to her. That was too risky, albeit very tempting. She had no intention of marrying him. No intention whatsoever of sleeping with him. If she did, he might expect more from her than she wanted to give. She didn't belong in Azzril anymore. She had a life in California. She couldn't compromise her plans, her freedom, by getting involved with the wrong man. A man very much like her father, set in his ways and strong in his beliefs. A man who had admitted he had no use for love in a relationship.

Then why did she sit up, cross her arms over her chest, slip the gown over her head and toss it onto the end of the bed? Why did she lay back, leaving the sheet at her feet? She had no explanation for her behavior, no reason to invite Dharr's attention. No rationale to be lying in a bed, practically naked, with a man who was more or less a stranger, worrying about whether or not he would touch her when she should be worrying about her father's health.

That was it. She was obviously on emotional overload, suffering from a lack of sensibility due to an abundance of concern. But from the beginning, she'd suspected Dharr hadn't been telling the complete truth about her father's condition. In fact, she was starting to wonder if the whole thing was a ploy to get her back home for a wedding—her wedding. Otherwise, if her papa had been in dire straits, someone would have called her. She could have made a few calls before she'd left Los Angeles to verify the information for herself.

Instead, she had agreed to get on a plane with Dharr Halim regardless of her suspicions, followed him on board without any coercion like a sheep following a shepherd. A seductive shepherd.

Reality hit her with the force of a sonic boom. Had she been waiting for Dharr Halim to show up on her doorstep? Is that why she'd been so eager to go with him? Would that explain why she'd had a number of boyfriends and a bevy of excuses for never making love with any of them? Her reasons had all seemed valid at the time. The dangers of indiscriminate sex in the form of sexually transmitted disease. Those boyfriends' lack of responsibility to anything aside from hedonistic pastimes, the next thrill. She'd been involved with men who'd been anything but safe and steady, committed. Mature.

Which begged the question—had she been saving herself for Dharr?

No. Her mind repelled that thought as she reached down for the sheet to cover herself. But before she could, Dharr's hand gripped her wrist. And if he dared to touch her, she wouldn't be able to resist him.

But he only drew the sheet up her body, as she'd intended to do.

"Turn to your side, facing the window," he commanded.

She readily complied, thinking that was probably wise. But when he fitted himself against her back and told her in a rough whisper to sleep, she didn't care about wisdom. Her attention was drawn to the feel of him against her—power and strength and heat. Scorching heat that seemed to flow through her, intense and unavoidable.

She highly doubted she would get any sleep this night. She also doubted that this foolish fascination with Dharr Halim would be gone in the morning.

A few hours before, Dharr had showered, dressed and joined his men in the main cabin downstairs to discuss business for a short while before returning to his quarters. At the moment he was seated in the chair near the bed while Raina still slept, unaware that he'd been watching her, captivated by her innocence, overwhelmed by his desire to make love with her.

He imagined in explicit detail exactly how he would begin—with his mouth trailing over her warm skin, lingering at her breasts, finding the heat between her thighs until she trembled with her own need. Then he would sink inside her, bringing her to a climax again…and again. He endeavored to keep that fantasy only that—a fantasy—for to do any more than imagine would test his honor. She was already testing his strength.

The captain's voice came over the intercom announcing the need to prepare for landing in London, forcing Dharr from his musings and startling Raina awake. She bolted upright, the sheet slipping to her waist. Her silky gold-brown hair veiled her breasts with the exception of one nipple peaking through a parting in her long locks.

Dharr shifted against the menace of another erection as he took in the sensual sight—until awareness dawned in her sleepy expression and she snatched the sheet back up to her chin.

"What's happening?" she asked in a grainy whisper.

Dharr considered showing her exactly what was happening to him but instead said, "We are about to land."

"In Azzril?"

"No. London to refuel. We will need to take our seats."

She glanced around the bed, lifting the sheet to look beneath it and giving Dharr another inadvertent view of her breasts. "Where's my gown?"

Dharr smiled and nodded toward the floor near the end of the bed. "It seems you are a very restless sleeper."

Concern replaced her frown and she gripped the sheet once more. "I didn't kick you out of bed, did I?"

In some ways, she had. "No."

"Do you mind handing it to me?"

He stood and approached the bed. "That is not necessary. You might wish to return to bed after we are on the ground. You might as well remain comfortable."

She inclined her head and sent him a coy look. "Are you suggesting I belt myself in naked?"

A prime suggestion at that. But the sound of the landing gear dropping spurred Dharr into action. Without thought, he leaned over and pulled the sheet from the mattress, tucked it securely around Raina and then scooped her from the bed. "We have little time to argue about your state of dress."

"Undress," she corrected. "And I can walk, Dharr."

Truthfully he wanted to feel her against him, at least for a few moments before he secured her into the seat. "You should save your energy."

She looked at him quizzically. "Save my energy for what?"

He considered several responses to that as he buckled himself in beside her. "For when you arrive in Azzril. You will need your strength to deal with your father."

"That's true. I might have to sit on him to make him be good."

Dharr considered asking her to sit on his lap so he could prove to her how good he could be before thrusting the hazardous thoughts away.

The plane rocked on its descent and Raina immediately gripped the edge of the seat. Determined to ease her distress, Dharr lifted the armrest between them, draped his arm around her and tipped her head against his shoulder.

"I'm really okay." She stiffened against him when the plane swayed again, belying her calm.

"It will be over soon," he assured her.

"Not soon enough," she said, her face turned into his neck.

Although he had thought not to repeat kissing her for his own sanity, Dharr decided doing so again might help her relax, even if it robbed him of his returning composure. On that thought, he tipped her chin up and pressed his lips to hers in a succession of soft, coaxing kisses. Without warning, she clasped his nape and pulled him closer, opening her mouth as if she regarded him as her lifeline.

Lost in her kiss, the gentle glide of her tongue against his, Dharr slid his hand down her back, taking the sheet with him as he guided his palm lower until he contacted the satin edging of her panties below the dip of her spine. How easy it would be to work his hand beneath the fabric. How easy it would be to keep going. To forget that anything existed beyond bringing her pleasure...

The plane bumped onto the runway, causing Dharr to pull

away from her mouth. Yet he could not quite find the will to remove his hand from her back, even after the plane taxied down the tarmac and came to a stop.

Raina stared up at him, eyes unfocused, lids heavy. "We're here," she murmured.

"Yes, we are," he said as slipped his palm beneath the satin to knead her buttocks without regard to caution.

"How long before…we're off again?"

Dharr feathered his fingertips over the smooth curves even knowing he must stop. The captain's voice announcing their arrival forced Dharr back into reality. Reluctantly he moved his hand away and set it in his lap. "We should be departing in less than an hour."

Raina collapsed back against the seat. "Do I have time to take a quick shower?"

The image of her naked and wet came to him clearly. "Certainly. If you are not quite ready when it's time to leave, I will ask for a short delay."

She smiled. "Oh, I'll let you know when I'm ready."

With that, she unbuckled the belt and slid from the seat, turning her back to him. The sheet gaped, revealing the slender path of her spine, the curve of her buttocks where he'd had his hand only moments before and above that, some sort of gold image embossed on the small of her back, something he had not noticed until that moment.

"What is that?" he asked.

She glanced over her shoulder and looked down. "It's a tattoo of a magic lamp." She raised her gaze to his. "Didn't you see it when you were spying on me at my house?"

"No." At that point, he'd been trying to avoiding anything that might have been deemed inappropriate, even though he had not been completely successful.

She faced him again. "You certainly had me fooled, considering you seemed to be bent on rubbing it a few minutes ago. I thought maybe you were making a wish."

Had he known, he would have wished for more strength, and a weaker libido.

Following a sultry look, Raina pulled a few toiletries from her bag and headed to the bathroom.

Dharr stared out the window, absently watching the activity on the tarmac below yet seeing only the image of Raina's body imprinted in his mind. He would like to see all of her, every fine fold, every soft crevice. How he would like to witness her face in the grip of a climax he had brought about.

Shifting against the building pressure, Dharr drew in a deep breath and made that wish for more fortitude—something he would need in the next few hours.

Three

Normally Raina wouldn't even attempt to wash her hair since it took so long to dry. But she wasn't feeling the least bit normal at the moment, the reason why she'd immersed herself completely beneath the shower spray.

How in the heck had she developed such a strong case of the hots for Dharr Halim? Why in the world had she let him touch her so intimately, kiss her so thoroughly? Of course, she had to concede that the depth of that kiss had been her fault. But the depth of her current need had been his. He was just too damn sexy for his own good—and hers.

She slicked her hand through her hair, washing away the remnants of conditioner, wishing she could wash away the fire sizzling through her body—from forehead to toes, gathering force between her legs. Definitely there.

After shutting off the faucet, Raina stepped outside the mini-shower onto the mat, fashioned a turban around her hair with one towel then dried off and wrapped up in another, knotting it between her breasts. Just then, the door opened to Dharr.

Raina sent him a not-so-nice look even though she had some really nice chills. "Do you mind giving me a little privacy?"

"Not at all." He stepped inside and closed the door behind him.

"Do you need something?" Raina asked.

His eyes burned black. "I thought perhaps I would shave since it seems we will be detained for a while longer."

Panic bit into Raina. "Is there something wrong with the plane?"

"Not the plane. The weather. Rain and heavy fog."

"Of course. It's London."

Raina stifled a gasp when Dharr unbuttoned his tailored shirt, slipped it off and hung it on a hook fastened to the door. She wanted to touch his broad bronzed chest, run her fingertips over the tensile ridges of masculine muscle, taste his nipples with her tongue. She gripped the edge of the towel at her thighs to keep from giving in to those urges.

As if unconcerned over her perusal, Dharr pulled out a razor and shaving cream from the cabinet. She watched as he smoothed the foam over his jaw with precision, recalling how good his hand had felt on her bottom. Imagining how good his hands would feel all over her extremely overheated body.

He studied her from the mirror's reflection. "Is there something you need from me?"

Yes, she did, but she didn't dare tell him exactly what she needed. "No. I'm just enjoying watching you shave. It reminds me of when I was a little girl. I used to stand in the bathroom while Papa shaved. He loved to give me a foamy moustache."

Taking Raina by surprise, Dharr reached back and streaked some of the cream across her upper lip. "Do you feel at home now?"

She couldn't stop her laughter as she pulled the towel from her hair and swiped the white foam away. "I feel a little silly since I'm no longer a girl."

His dark eyes went darker, hotter as he focused on her breasts barely concealed by the towel. "I have noticed."

Raina noticed how with only a look, he could make her dissolve into a she-devil. "I guess I'll go get dressed now."

"What a pity."

She slapped him with the towel across his very tight butt encased in form-fitting slacks. "You are still a relentless tease, Dharr Halim."

"And you are a great temptation, Raina Kahlil. Almost more than I can withstand."

"I find that hard to believe, a big strong man like you."

Their gazes remained fixed in the mirror's reflection for a long moment until Raina decided she best get out of there before she suggested they initiate Dharr's onboard miniscule boudoir—standing up against the wall.

"I'll see you later," she said, then worked her way behind him. The small space allowed for little room to maneuver and her breasts brushed across his broad back. Her nipples tightened into hard knots against the towel and Dharr nicked himself, creating a trickle of blood streaming down his chin.

"I'm sorry," Raina said as she grabbed for a tissue, reached around him and dabbed at the cut, her front pressed against his back.

"I can handle a slight injury." Without turning around, Dharr clasped her wrist, tossed aside the tissue and drew her palm down his chest, down his abdomen and lower until she contacted the hard crest straining against his slacks. "This is more difficult to ignore."

Raina's breath hitched as she fought the urge to explore him, to know the details even if the slacks provided a hindrance to really experience all that power. But before she gave into the impulse, he pulled her hand back up to his chest. "Now leave before I am tempted to put that to good use."

Stunned into silence, Raina hurried out of the bathroom, closed the door and leaned against it. Her legs trembled. Her whole body trembled. She wanted him with an all-consuming need that challenged wisdom. She wanted to know exactly what it would be like to make love with him.

But she really shouldn't, for that kind of intimacy might bring with it bared emotions. She didn't want to feel anything for him beyond friendship. She didn't want to get caught up in his sensual web and find herself entangled to the point she couldn't break free.

If she thought she could be assured that she could keep all emotion out of it, she wouldn't hesitate to cross the limits just so she could know. But then, maybe she was stronger than she thought. So was Dharr Halim. And she probably wouldn't be any match for his kind of strength.

Admittedly the sheikh was a fantasy man. Her fantasy man. Not until now had she realized how true that had been most of her life. During her secret, intimate imaginings, he had appeared more than once even though she'd tried to force the images away. Even though she'd been little more than a child when she'd seen him the last time, she'd never forgotten him. She'd never forgotten his smile, his aura, his sheer masculine beauty. Maybe it was time to make the fantasy reality. She knew he would treat her with care if they made love. She knew he would be the perfect man to be her first lover.

When this journey ended, they would go on living separate lives. And after she saw to her father's recovery, she would return to America with a few good memories—if Dharr Halim was willing to give her those, and more.

* * *

After the hour delay had turned into four, Dharr and Raina had dined together, talking in generalities about her life in California, his work on Azzril's economy and the changes they had both encountered over the years. All the while, Dharr had silently cursed himself for his weakness where Raina was concerned. He'd barely been able to concentrate on conversation due to his fascination with her mouth. She'd seemed totally unaware of the effect she had on him. However, after the warning he'd given her in the bathroom, she should have no doubt. And he'd had no shame in showing her, something he hoped he would not regret. Yet since she had boarded his plane, he had been quick to toss away common sense or courtesy, for that matter. He had to remember who she was—the daughter of his father's best friend, a woman who should be shown the utmost respect. A woman who held too much power over his attention at the moment. At any given moment.

Right then she sat on the bed, legs crossed, pencil and paper in hand, creating something he could not see from his vantage point in the chair. But he could see the fullness of her unencumbered breasts outlined in detail against the tight knit top, and that alone kept pulling his attention away from the newspaper he pretended to be reading.

The phone attached to the wall shrilled, sending him out of his chair to answer the summons. As suspected, it was the call he'd requested.

He held out the receiver and told Raina, "It is for you."

She looked up from her drawing and frowned. "Who is it?"

"Come and see."

She set the paper aside and slipped off the bed, the gauzy pants she now wore flowing with every step she took, accentuating her pleasing shape and her grace as she crossed to

where Dharr was standing. She gave him another questioning look before taking the receiver and saying, "Hello?"

When she smiled, Dharr felt her joy as keenly as if it were
his own. "Papa? How are you?"

After reclaiming his seat, he tried not to eavesdrop on the
conversation but was surprised to hear her converse with her
father in fluent Arabic, as if she spoke it daily. At least he
could be assured she would have no trouble communicating
once they returned to Azzril. He, on the other hand, could have
a great deal of trouble keeping his hands to himself even after
they arrived in his country.

He continued to watch her, enthralled by the way she
twined one lock of hair around her finger, her expressive eyes,
her bouts of laughter.

"Yes, Sheikh Halim is taking good care of me, Papa," she
said as she sent Dharr a brief look of appreciation. He would
like to please her more before their travels ended, although
he did not dare knowing that nothing more would exist between them. And that was beginning to work on Dharr in ways
he could not comprehend.

Granted, Raina Kahlil could be deemed a suitable candi-
date for future queen considering her legacy. And she was
beautiful. Intelligent. Young and vibrant. Any man would be
honored to have her as his wife.

Yet Dharr acknowledged that Raina would be reluctant to
consider settling into that role—unless he could somehow
convince her that certain advantages did exist should they decide to adhere to the marriage terms. Then he promptly realized he was trying to convince himself of that very thing.

He rejected that notion altogether. Primal attraction was the
only thing that existed between them at present, even if he
found her to be interesting, and exciting beyond all bounds.
He could not let down his guard and entertain anything but

fondness for her knowing she would not stay with him. Knowing she had a life in America that would not include him.

Before she hung up the phone, Dharr moved onto the bed and picked up the drawing to find she had sketched a good likeness of him, including the scowl he had most surely been sporting.

"You weren't supposed to see that yet," she said from above him.

He regarded her over one shoulder. "You are very talented, but I do not believe I look this serious."

She sat down beside him. "Yes, you do. Most of the time. I'm assuming that stoic demeanor is in part because of your duty."

In part because of duty and in part because of his unanswered desire for her. "I do not take my responsibility lightly." The reason he could not act on that desire.

She balanced her heels on the edge of the bed and hugged her knees to her breasts. "I know. And thank you for the phone call."

Her closeness created another fire that burned low in his belly. "Is your father well?"

"Yes. And why didn't you tell me he was staying at the palace when he has a perfectly good mansion of his own?"

"He has limited company and very few servants. I felt it best he be attended to by my staff, including my physician."

"I appreciate your kindness more than you know."

Dharr appreciated every nuance of her beautiful face, every vibrant smile. "You are welcome. And my apologies for the delay in our journey."

She shrugged. "That's not your fault. You have no control over the weather."

"True, but I know you are anxious to see your father."

She collapsed back onto the bed, her hair forming a halo around her face. "If not for him, I wouldn't be so ready to leave. I don't mind this plane when it's not moving."

Dharr shifted where he could see her better. "Have you had a bad experience before?"

"Do you mean with flying?"

"Yes. Something that brought on your fear."

She stared at the low ceiling. "The night I left Azzril with my mother, it was stormy. The flight was bumpy all the way to the States. I was terrified."

Her tone more than proved that to Dharr, but he had other suspicions in terms of her fear. "And you were leaving your home."

Her gaze came to rest on his. "Yes. Leaving my papa and at the time, I really didn't know why."

"Did your mother not explain? Did she not comfort you?"

Raina sat again and clutched a pillow to her chest, as if she needed the security. "She was zoned out most of the trip and for weeks after that. At first she told me we were only in California temporarily, then she finally told me we wouldn't be back in Azzril."

The abject pain in her voice disturbed Dharr. "That must have been difficult for you."

She shrugged. "I managed. But my life's been a breeze compared to yours."

"In what way?"

"You're an only son, Dharr. You've been groomed to eventually rule a country, no questions asked."

"I have always accepted my duty and all that it entails."

She appeared doubtful. "But you went to college in the States. You must've enjoyed your freedom during that time. No responsibilities except making the grade."

Odd that she seemed to understand him so well. "I only had limited freedom. The press was relentless."

"That's true. I remember Mother showing me pictures of you in magazines and the newspapers. I especially recall a few times when I saw you keeping company with some socialite named Elizabeth something or other."

Dharr internally flinched over hearing the name. "I am surprised you would have been interested in my private life."

"Of course I was interested. She was on the arm of my presumed future husband." She smiled around her sarcasm. "Do you two still keep in touch?"

Dharr had no cause—or desire—to revisit the past. "I believe it would be best if we agree not to question each other over former relationships."

"Obviously dear Elizabeth is a touchy subject. But it's a deal. No talk about past loves."

"I never said that I loved her." Even though he had.

"Whatever you say, Sheikh Halim. You keep your secrets and I'll keep mine."

The only secrets Dharr wanted to know about Raina Kahlil had to do with her response if he made love with her. Even though she'd brought back the bitter memories, his focus was still on the woman he'd known as girl all those years ago. Even now he would gladly climb into the bed with her, divest them of clothing and learn her well. Yet honor prevented him from doing so.

Dharr rubbed his eyes in an attempt to erase the visions and when he opened them, he found Raina frowning.

"You look tired," she said. "Did you get any sleep at all?"

"Some."

After repositioning the pillow, she laid back and patted the place beside her. "Come here. We can take a nap while we're waiting for this heap to get off the ground again."

Every instinct Dharr owned shouted danger. "Perhaps that is not such a good idea."

"Come on, Dharr. We have on clothes. It's no big deal."

He was not that weak. He could lie down with her and do

nothing more, or so he hoped. "I suppose you are right." He stretched out on his back beside her, one arm lying rigid at his side, the other bent beneath his head in an effort not to touch her.

Yet Raina greatly complicated matters when she curled up close to his side and rested her cheek on his chest. Something deep within Dharr began to dissolve. The warmth that flowed through him had only partially to do with carnal cravings. Feelings he did not care to allow threatened to surface. Yet when she tipped her face up and whispered, "You smell great. You feel good, too," all his resistance fled as he drew her mouth to his.

Once more he gave in to his need for her, culminating in a kiss that began tenderly before turning deeper. Dharr framed her face in his palms, drawing on her heat, her essence. Their limbs became entwined as they explored each other with their hands, avoiding places that would send them effectively over the edge.

Then Raina slid her hands down his back to his buttocks and nudged him over until he was completely atop her. Though their clothes provided a substantial obstacle, the movement of Raina's hips beneath him created a friction that encouraged his desire despite his determination to keep his body at bay. Now only the true act of lovemaking could bring them closer.

As badly as Dharr wanted that very thing, he recognized the peril in continuing. In a matter of moments, he would not be able to stop. He would strip her clothes from her, remove his own clothes then take this interlude beyond the restrictions he'd purposely posed.

Mustering what little strength he had left, Dharr pushed away from Raina and sat on the edge of the bed, keeping his back to her. He could hear her ragged breathing that echoed his own then felt her hand on his back.

"Dharr, I think we should just give up."

He rested his elbows on his knees, lowered his head and streaked both hands over his face. "I do not understand what you are saying." A lie. He knew exactly what she was saying, and exactly what she wanted from him. He wanted it, as well, badly. But his head argued against that even though his body refused to listen.

She worked her way beside him and took his hand into hers. "We should give up pretending we don't want each other and just let whatever happens, happen."

He straightened and gathered all the arguments. "I would not want to dishonor you by making love with you without any commitment."

She smiled, a cynical one. "Dishonor me? This is not ancient times. We're both consenting adults."

"And you would be satisfied with only sex?"

"Yes, of course." Her tone sounded tentative, yet her expression appeared resolute. "I don't see why we can't just follow nature's lead. If we wanted to take a little pleasure in each other, why shouldn't we?"

She skimmed her fingertips up and down his arm, fueling his hunger for her once more when he imagined her hands beneath his slacks, doing the same.

For the sake of his own sanity, he bolted from the bed and faced her.

"I cannot forget who I am, Raina, or my responsibility. I promised your father I would see you safely to Azzril. He would not approve if I took advantage of this situation by allowing any more intimacy between us. I have already done enough."

She worked her way from the bed and stood before him, close enough to touch him. "I know all too well who you are, Dharr. But don't you ever wish you could forget for a while?

I know I do. I mean, I've been my mother's rock for ten years. I lived with her, supported her, basically baby-sat her until I moved out recently. For once I just want to let go. Do something I want to do."

"I cannot afford to do that."

She folded her arms across her chest and presented a look of defiance. "What not? Because you're supposed to be some superhuman without feelings or needs or desires? I know you have desires, Dharr. You've been playing games with me since we walked onto this plane. You stripped out of your clothes and crawled into bed with me last night. A few hours ago, you took my hand and you showed me how much you wanted me. You've been engaging in a tug-of-war and you're afraid to admit you're losing."

Dharr recognized the truth in her words even though he did not care for it. "I am a man, Raina, and I admit I have done things I should not have done. Yet I must stop before we go past the point of no return."

She smoothed a hand down his chest. "I think we've already gone past that point, Dharr. We went past it the first time you kissed me. You know it. And I know it, too."

He pressed his palm against her fingers, intending to take her hand away. Instead he held it against his pounding heart. "Again, it would not be fair to you. Since both of us do not intend to uphold our marriage contract, we would have no commitment to each other. If we are to make that clear to our fathers, then it would be unwise to continue on this path."

She moved closer, almost flush against him. "No one would have to know what goes on between us on this plane. After we're in Azzril, it would be our secret."

It was no secret he wanted her; that much Dharr could not deny. Yet he considered another pressing issue aside from the one beneath his slacks. "Even if I did decide to consider what you are saying, I have nothing on board to protect you from pregnancy."

She frowned. "That could be a problem since a child is something neither one of us needs."

Finally she was seeing the logic in what he was saying. "So now you understand the risk and why we cannot proceed."

Her smile appeared, slow and sultry. "We could if we didn't completely make love. There are other ways we could enjoy each other without the actual act. I'm sure you know more than a few."

He did and the temptation to show her was almost overwhelming. "You deserve much more, Raina."

She circled her arms around his neck. "We deserve to have this time together, Dharr. We deserve to lock out the world and forget about everything but each other. I dare you to be only the man, not the preeminent prince, for the next few hours we have together."

Framing her face in his palms, he tipped his forehead against hers. "You are testing my strength, Raina."

She pulled one of his hands to her breast. "I intend to do more than that to you."

Tossing all caution aside, Dharr claimed her mouth again in another heated exchange, fierce and fiery and in many ways, forbidden. He fondled her breast, tested her nipple with his fingertips through the thin material. He lowered the top's strap and left her mouth to kiss her shoulder, all the while warnings raging in his head. Yet he was helpless in her presence. The man wanted her without hesitation; the prince argued against the wisdom in that.

The man won out as he began to back her to the bed.

The rap on the door jolted Dharr from the erotic haze and sent him away from Raina. Storming to the entry on the heels of his frustration, he opened the door only enough to see the intruder, his senior staff member, Abid Raneer.

"What is it?" Dharr's tone sounded gruff and impatient despite his attempts at remaining calm.

Abid nodded. "Forgive the intrusion, but the captain wishes to speak with you, Sheikh Halim."

"I will be there in a moment."

Without another word, Dharr closed the door on his assistant and leaned back against it for support.

Raina was seated on the edge of the bed, her arms crossed over her breasts, which did nothing to quell Dharr's desire. "Is something wrong?"

Yes, Dharr decided. He was as hard as granite and that would not be easy to conceal. "I have been summoned downstairs. I will return as soon as possible."

"Okay."

When he made no move to leave, Raina asked, "Are you going?"

"I need a few more moments."

She sent her gaze to his distended fly, making matters worse. "I see."

And so would his men. "I would greatly appreciate your absence for a few moments. Perhaps you should retrieve a drink from the galley."

Her grin appeared, teasing and tempting. "You're going to leave me quivering with need? Hot for your body? Ready to jump all over you and tear off your clothes?"

Raina," he cautioned. "If you continue with that talk, I will be further delayed and you will have to wait longer for my return."

"Then you're going to consider what I'm proposing?" She sounded hopeful, and determined.

"We will discuss it as soon as I come back."

She smiled victoriously then pointed behind her. "I'll just go see what I can find in the fridge."

Dharr heard her soft laughter and the pad of her footsteps as she walked away. He willed his body to quiet, willed the return to restraint even though he recognized that when he walked back through the door, back to her, all restraint would be gone again.

Four

After ten minutes of staring at the ceiling, Raina decided that Dharr had reconsidered and caught another plane. If she hadn't recognized the total absence of logic, she might have panicked. She wasn't sure how she would continue this flight without him.

Of course she could do it. She didn't need his distractions, or at least she didn't want to need them. He'd already distracted her so much that she'd tossed away all her good sense for an opportunity that could prove to be very risky. But she'd never been afraid of taking chances; no need to begin now.

First, she had to have the man back, and she got her wish when the door opened and Dharr stepped into the room.

"What's going on?" she asked when she noted his stony expression.

"Nothing momentous," Dharr said as he closed the door behind him. "Only that we are about to take off again."

Raina only wanted to take off his clothes, and hers. Dharr seemed intent on preparing for departure when he sat in the designated seat. "Come. We will be leaving in a matter of moments."

Resigned that she had to do this, she took the seat next him for the familiar routine. She secured her seat belt, he fastened his own then wrapped his arm around her shoulder to pull her close to his side.

Raina couldn't deny the thrill of being next to him once more, hoping that after they got the journey underway again, he would be more accommodating. If she survived the take-off. She despised this part most of all. Dharr knew that well, evident by his soft lips trailing kisses along her jaw as the engines revved up and the plane reversed.

Raina risked a glance out the window to notice the rain still pounding the plastic pane. "Are you sure we should be leaving?" Her tone sounded high and wary.

"It is safe," Dharr whispered as he smoothed his palm up her bare arm. "You are in good hands."

Raina couldn't argue that point since Dharr's "good hands" breezing up the side of her breast had turned her insides into the consistency of oatmeal. But when the plane shook as they left the runway, even Dharr's caresses couldn't prevent the fear weighting her chest.

She buried her face into his neck and muttered, "I hate this. I hate being afraid."

With gentle fingertips, Dharr tipped her face up. "Look at me," he said, his tone commanding. "You have nothing to fear with me."

Oh, but she did. She feared the feelings he stirred within her, the urge to totally let go. She feared giving everything to him. Feared she wouldn't want to leave him when the time came to go back to her life, but not enough to put a halt to her plans even though he had yet to agree to her proposition.

"Take off your blouse," he whispered when the plane pitched as it banked to the right.

Her mouth dropped open from utter shock before awareness dawned and she leveled her gaze on his. "You've changed your mind." She posed the words as affirmation, not a question, because she could see surrender in his dark, dark eyes.

"You need distraction and I am going to give that to you."

Distraction she could definitely use but she hoped it wasn't temporary. "I'll take off mine if you take off yours."

"I see you are bent on bargaining with me for the remainder of this flight." Fortunately for Raina, he didn't sound angry. He did sound sexy as hell.

"That depends on how cooperative you're going to be from here on out."

He hinted at a smile while he released the buttons on his shirt. "That remains to be seen although I greatly question my wisdom."

"To heck with wisdom." Drawing in a deep breath, Raina crossed her arms, clasped the hem and pulled the top over her head. And now here they were, Dharr bare-chested and beautiful and she nude to the waist.

Once more he curled his arm over one shoulder, using his free hand to push her hair away and cup her breast lightly. "You are very tempting," he said. "Very beautiful."

Raina could barely draw a breath, much less manage a thank you. And her oxygen level decreased severely when he dipped his head and drew a nipple into the wet warmth of his expert mouth. She slid her hands into his hair and closed her eyes, the turbulent take-off all but forgotten, replaced by a host of sensations provoked by Dharr's soft suckling.

As he continued to mesmerize her, he traced the silver

loop at her navel with a leisurely fingertip, enticing and exciting her into mindlessness. Yet he didn't make even the slightest move to lower his hand. He simply continued to draw random designs on her belly above where the belt rested low on her lap, laving his tongue across her nipple a final time before working his way up her neck and to her ear.

"When we are cleared to leave these seats, do you know what I wish to do?" He spoke in a low whisper, his warm breath filtering over her neck.

"What?"

He traced the silver loops in her lobe with his tongue. "I am going to take you to the bed."

"To sleep?"

"To touch you. To learn every inch of you, if that is what you still want from me."

"Promise?"

"You may count on it."

Raina counted the seconds until he would make good on his promise. Waited for someone to tell them they could get out of the blasted seats.

When that didn't immediately happen, Dharr rested his hand on her thigh, rubbing his knuckles back and forth on the inside of her leg. Overcome with her own need to know how affected he might be, Raina slid her palm up his thigh and back down again, moving closer and closer to his groin each time.

"You are entering dangerous territory, Raina."

She grinned. "What's wrong with being a little dangerous?"

He brushed a kiss across her lips then pulled her hand back to his chest. "I am entitled to my turn first. Orders from the sheikh."

He prevented Raina from leveling any kind of come-back when he kissed her again, using his tongue like a feather while he slipped his hand between her thighs, applied a slight pressure there, bringing about a rush of wet heat. Raina was only slightly aware of the rocking plane as she concentrated on Dharr's distraction. His touch served as her only reality at the moment and one she never wanted to leave, at least not yet. Not until she experienced the limits of Dharr's skills, although she truly suspected there were no limits to what he would do to make a woman feel good. He was doing it to her now.

When Raina made a small sound of need, Dharr balanced on the threshold of madness. Yet he reminded himself that he did intend to take this slowly should they change their mind. And that was about as likely as either of them pursuing the marriage arrangement.

Dharr kissed her breasts again, then went back to her mouth, playing his tongue against hers in meaningful strokes, caressing her through the thin fabric of her pants, indicating what he would do to her body if given the chance to completely make love with her. And though that chance would not come on this plane, he would still give her the greatest pleasure she had ever known, or die trying.

The bell sounded and the fasten seat belt sign went out, causing Raina to tense, effectively interrupting their interlude.

Dharr took her hand into his and studied her flushed face. "Are you certain you want to continue this, Raina?"

She squeezed his hand tightly. "Yes. Unless you don't."

"I want it," he said. "Very unwise, I know, but this need I have for you makes very little sense."

She smiled. "Maybe we shouldn't worry about being sensible. After all, what else are we going to do to pass the time?"

The humor in her tone contrasted with Dharr's lack of mirth, yet he would always remember Raina's smile, no matter what the future held. "I suppose you are right, although most people would take that time to sleep."

She reached over and unfastened his seat belt, brushing her

fingertips across his increasing erection. "We're not most people, Dharr."

Dharr could not argue that point even though the debate in his mind continued over whether he should allow this tryst. Yet when Raina leaned over and whispered, "I believe our bed's waiting," all questions and concerns drifted away.

Standing, he held out his hand to her and she took it without hesitation. Once they made it to the bed, Dharr vowed to remain in command. Yet he could not resist kissing her without restraint. A long, deep kiss. A prelude to what would come.

Once they parted, Dharr could not discern who was more winded. He locked into Raina's golden eyes and told her, "We will take this slowly."

She frowned. "If we go too slowly, I'll go crazy."

"I plan for you to do that very thing."

"I'm looking forward to it."

"Now lie facedown on the bed."

She sent him a quizzing look. "May I ask why?"

He brushed her hair back from her breasts and leaned to take another brief taste. "You may ask, but you will have to wait and see. I will only say that if we are going to go forward with this, I intend to do it well."

"I'm going to hold you to that."

He drew a line down her jaw with a fingertip. "Trust me, Raina. I am not going to hurt you in any way. And anything that I do to you that you do not care for, you only need tell me and I will stop."

Her smile appeared, a bit shaky yet still a smile. "I trust you."

He wasn't certain he trusted himself to stop when necessary. "Good. Now on the bed."

When she reached for the drawstring on her pants, Dharr clasped her wrist. "Not yet. I will take care of that later."

"Okay, as long as you do."

While she climbed onto the bed onto her belly, Dharr set about lowering the shades on the windows and turning down all the lights except for the one above the bed that cast Raina in a sensual glow. He then opened one of the built-in cabinets and retrieved a bottle of massage oil.

After squeezing a few drops into his palm, Dharr sat on the edge of the bed, the bottle braced between his knees. He paused a moment to survey the golden lamp peeking from the waistband of Raina's pants, seriously doubting that the sultan knew his daughter had permanently marked her body, nor did he believe her father would approve. Dharr also recognized that her father would disapprove of what they were about to do.

Pushing those thoughts aside, he told her, "Pull your hair away from your back." Once she complied, he started the first part of the journey by spreading the oil across her shoulders.

"What is that heavenly smell?" she asked in a languid tone, her words muffled by the pillow where she'd buried her face. Eventually he would request that she watch what he was doing, but not quite yet.

"It is plumeria oil."

She lifted her head and looked back at him. "Massage oil, huh? And you tried to tell me you've never had a woman on board."

"The past shall be kept in the past, Raina." He bent and kissed her cheek. "What matters now are the hours we have together. Only us and no one else."

"You're right. I'm sorry." She laid her cheek back against the pillow. "Now carry on."

Exactly what Dharr planned to do. With calculated caresses, he worked his way down her back, curling his fingertips around her sides and using his thumbs to track the fine beads of her spine. When he reached the tattoo, he leaned down to kiss the spot before continuing his downward progress.

He slid his hands beneath her belly, tugging the drawstring to loosen the material and to provide access to all of her body. He smiled when she lifted her hips, allowing him to lower the pants slowly, taking her panties with them until he had them pushed to her thighs. The sight of her taut buttocks, the feel of her soft skin beneath his palms, only served to threaten his patience. But he refused to hurry this exploration, for both their sakes. Impatience could prove detrimental to his control. He could not allow that to happen.

Once more he dipped his head to apply a kiss, this time on each buttock then lightly flicked his tongue along the cleft. Raina's gasp brought his gaze back to her where he found her hands fisted tightly on the pillow.

After he worked the pants completely away and tossed them aside, he bracketed her hips and said, "Turn over."

She did as he asked, her breasts rising and falling in anticipation of what would come next. And what he planned for her would also prevent normal respiration, as soon as she was ready.

On that thought, Dharr propped two pillows beneath her shoulders then took the oil and placed a few more drops in his palm. He applied the liquid to her slender neck before working his way to the rise of her breasts.

"Watch, Raina," he whispered as he circled her nipples with his fingertips. The oil had created a fine satin sheen over her skin; his fondling had created a glaze in her eyes.

"That feels so good," she murmured, her voice low as if speaking took great effort.

Dharr paused to ply her lips with soft teasing kisses, pleased when each time they parted, Raina raised her head to seek his mouth once more.

"Do you wish to feel better?" he asked after pulling away

from her lips, suffering from the loss yet knowing he would eventually return there.

"By all means."

"Then you shall."

He skimmed his hands down her abdomen, spreading more of the floral oil in his wake before he paused to play with the silver ring in her navel. He found that jewelry quite intriguing. He found every inch of her intriguing, from her thick silky hair to her pink painted toenails.

Only then did he allow himself to study the shading between her thighs, knowing that in doing so, he would become excruciatingly hard at the sight, and he did. Yet his own needs would not take precedence over hers.

After applying more oil to his palm then setting the bottle on the floor, he bent her legs toward her hips. He sent his hand over her knee, down her well-toned calf and to her delicate ankle then did the same to her other leg. He moved almost to the end of the bed and nudged her thighs apart, leaving her open to his eyes.

When Raina laid her hand on her abdomen, for a fleeting moment he believed she might try to cover herself. Yet she didn't. She did continue to stare at him, expectancy in her expression, heat in her eyes.

He now faced a certain dilemma—would he use his hands or his mouth to give her pleasure? He would like nothing better than to test her with his tongue, an act that would be deemed one of the most intimate between a man and a woman. Perhaps he should avoid that level of intimacy. He had to remember that after they left the privacy of this plane, nothing else would come of this liaison.

He moved onto his knees between her legs and with both hands, pressed downward strokes from her navel toward her pubis, stimulating the blood flow to heighten her orgasm, as he had learned long ago. Lower and lower he traveled, through the shading of hair until he parted the soft pleats to reveal his ultimate goal. He swirled a fingertip round and round her swollen flesh, watching her face grow slack with every caress.

When Raina lifted her hips, encouraging him toward his mark, he quickened his pace, applied more pressure, knowing that she was coming closer to a climax. He guided one finger inside her to experience the waves of spasms, imagining her surrounding him yet knowing he must settle for only this.

A soft moan hissed out of her mouth and she bit her lower lip as he continued to touch her again and again, intent on giving her another release. But she grabbed his wrist and pulled him forward atop her before he could continue.

"Did I hurt you?" he asked, his voice hoarse from his current position between her legs. He would only have to lower his fly and shove down his briefs to thrust inside her.

"Do I look like I'm in pain?"

She looked beautiful in the aftermath of her fulfillment, but he was definitely in pain. "I want to touch you again."

"No." She worked her way from beneath him and nudged him aside. "Now it's my turn, Dharr."

As much as Dharr wanted her hands on him, he still feared a total loss of restraint, something he could not afford. Right now he was bordering on throwing caution to the wind to bury himself inside her. If she touched him, he would have to rely on solid sense to remind him why they could not end this interlude with true consummation. "That is not necessary. This time we have left I promised to dedicate solely to your pleasure."

Without regard to his words, she rolled onto her side to face him and reached for his fly to lower his zipper. "Yes, it is necessary. For me. Now take off your clothes so we'll be even, or I'll be glad to do it for you."

As far as Dharr was concerned, the odds were stacked against him, even more so when she stroked him through his briefs. Caution be damned, he would allow her to touch him, at least for a time. He would endeavor to hold back although that prospect seemed challenging. But he would face that when the time came.

Leaving the bed and her intoxicating touch, he removed his pants and briefs then stood before her, allowing her to see exactly how she had affected him. The increasing pressure between his legs only grew worse as her gaze traveled over his body.

She smiled and tapped one finger against her chin. "Well, you are certainly happy to see me."

He moved a step closer to the bed at his own peril. "Do you find everything to your liking?"

She continued to study him with a total lack of inhibition. "I would say you're definitely a ten."

A sudden surge of jealousy hurled through Dharr. "In comparison to whom?"

She rose to her knees before him and flattened her palms against his chest. "I'm not comparing you to anyone, Dharr. Remember, the past is in the past."

He did not appreciate having his words thrown back at him even though he admitted she was right. Still, the thought of another man making love to her only fueled his determination to prove himself. If he could not be her first, he would most certainly be her best.

Nudging Raina back onto the bed, Dharr stretched out to face her and gently rolled her taut nipple between his forefinger and thumb. "What would you have me do now? I am open to any request. Or perhaps you would wish me to choose."

She ran both hands down his chest, following the stream of hair before pausing at his abdomen. "I expect you to let me have my turn."

He gritted his teeth when she circled her fingertip around his navel. "Again, I am not certain that is wise."

"Wise or not, I'm going to do it. Now let me have some of that oil."

He hesitated a brief moment in recognition that if he gave into her whims, he could be in for heaven mixed with hell. But he would allow her the opportunity since he did not have the strength to fight her on the issue. He'd been in a steady state of arousal since their first encounter. He only hoped he could maintain some semblance of self-discipline.

Reaching behind him, he retrieved the bottle and squeezed a coin-sized dab into her open palm. "That's not very much," she said.

"A little goes a very long way." How very true. Being so close to her went a long way toward stealing Dharr's resolve to stay strong.

At first her touch was tentative, nothing more than a fingertip breezing down his length as she watched with fascination. She grew bolder with her discovery, yet somewhat hesitant at times, leading him to wonder if perhaps she had never touched a man this way before. He only wished that were true. Then she took him completely into her oil-slicked hands, her movements more deliberate—and deadly to Dharr.

Robbed of his will, he tossed the bottle of oil into the floor, not caring if he'd closed the lid. He only cared about Raina's tempered stroking and enthusiastic exploration. Other women had touched him this way yet not exactly this way, with such thoroughness and curiosity.

Tipping his forehead against hers, he lowered his eyes to watch her ministrations, knowing that by doing so he would only create more havoc on his resolve to allow this only for a while. A long breath hissed out from between his clenched teeth when she swirled one thumb over the sensitive tip several times.

With the last of his waning strength, he said, "Stop."

"No." She defied him not only verbally but also by quickening her pace.

He pulled her closer, his hips surging in time with her cadence. It was too much, yet not enough. "Not this way."

"There isn't another way."

Lost to her touch, he uttered the next thought that came to mind. "I want to be inside you."

"You know you can't," she said in a breathless whisper.

Dharr realized that all too well. Realized that in a matter of moments, self-control would desert him and he would have no choice than to let go completely. He'd been a fool to think he could begin to stop it, or Raina.

All sound disappeared save the rasp of his breath, or perhaps it was hers. He soon arrived at the place where coherent thought collided with sensation. Where logic retreated and primal instinct took over. He had no claim on his body, no power to fight the rush. The climax came with striking potency, bringing with it rigorous release, then welcome relief. And finally, awareness.

For only the second time in Dharr Halim's life, he was totally powerless—and completely enslaved—by a woman. And he realized she could hold the key to keeping him that way for the remainder of their journey, if not longer.

Raina left the shower and returned to the cabin, inhaling the pungent aroma of the exotic floral scents combined with sex lingering still, though she'd washed the remnants away from her skin. But she couldn't rid herself of the memory of Dharr's hands on her only a few hours before, or what she had done to him. Nor could she ignore that she only had an hour left before recollections of an incredible experience with a highly sensual man were all that remained.

She had no idea what he thought of her now. He had no idea that she'd never touched a man the way she'd touched him. True, she had seen her share of male anatomy in art classes when she'd painted nudes, and she'd dated several men who had attempted to persuade her into their beds or the back seat of their cars. Not one had ever tempted her enough to totally let go of all inhibitions—until Dharr Halim.

Tucking the towel securely between her breasts and tightening the ponytail high atop her head, Raina tiptoed past the bed where Dharr still slept. She had every intention of getting dressed before waking him, but she was drawn to the glorious scene laid out atop the rumpled sheets—one beautifully nude man lying on his stomach, one arm casually resting over his head, the other across the place she'd left minutes before.

His hair was sufficiently tousled—and sexy, but then so was the rest of his amazing body. From the hue of his cocoa-colored skin to the backs of his hair spattered thighs, he was undeniably gorgeous. And his butt—well, Raina couldn't find the words to express the splendor of that.

When he stirred slightly and turned his face toward her, she took a seat on the edge of the bed and laid a hand on his back. "Dharr, are you awake?"

He didn't respond or open his eyes so she stretched out beside him, lifting his arm and draping it over her middle. Raina assumed he was still asleep, allowing her the opportunity to look her fill a while longer. His dark lashes fanned out below his closed eyes and a shadow of whiskers surrounded his sensuous lips—lips that she wanted to kiss again and again and again. But as soon as they walked off this godforsaken plane, that wouldn't be possible. Everything that had happened between them to this point would have to be kept secret, and it couldn't happen again. Not if they wanted to keep up the pretense that they were only friends and not destined to marry, regardless of their fathers' wishes. Only she found herself wishing…

No. That was totally absurd. She and Dharr might be united by cultural heritage, but they lived two very different lives. She wouldn't be happy in Azzril, and he sure as heck wouldn't be traveling to California to see her. Half a world separated them by distance; a whole universe divided them in terms of their goals. It simply wouldn't work between them even if she inherently knew how well they worked in bed, albeit in a limited sense. She also knew that if protection from pregnancy had been readily available, she would have known everything—how it would have felt to have him inside her. Now she would probably never know.

Feeling somewhat melancholy, Raina resigned herself to what had to be and decided to dress. But she barely moved an inch before Dharr pulled her closer and buried his face in her exposed neck. He radiated heat like a potter's kiln and he still smelled like the oil she'd personally applied to his body.

Raina shivered from the sudden sexual awareness, the onslaught of an unfathomable need for him. Only him. Without saying a word, he lavished her neck with light kisses, abrading her skin with his beard though she really didn't feel it much. She did feel his hardness pressing against her pelvis, felt the damp heat between her thighs in response. In her logical mind, she recognized she should stop him before they went any further. In her heart of hearts, she didn't have the desire to do that. And when he flicked open the knotted terry cloth with one finger, any and all objections went the way of the towel he pulled from beneath her and tossed onto the ground.

His warm mouth closed over her nipple while he fondled her other breast with slightly callused fingertips. So attuned to what Dharr was doing to her, she was only mildly aware that he'd nudged her legs apart. But soon she became very aware that he had slid his hand down to guide his erection between her legs, much too close to the point of no return.

She needed to stop him, *had* to stop him *now*. But before she could articulate her concerns, he rolled off her and onto his back, one arm covering his eyes.

"Get dressed, Raina." His tone was harsh, authoritative.

"I will, but first we should—"

"Get dressed before I do something we both regret."

Raina only regretted that they hadn't been able to completely make love. As she snatched up the discarded towel, then her bag and returned to the bathroom, she couldn't stop the sudden sour mood.

For the next few days, she would go to bed alone until the time came for her to return home. She would not be able to enjoy his kisses, lose herself in his touch or to touch him. Would never know how it would be to have him fill her completely. Worse, they would walk around pretending that nothing had happened between them.

But something had happened to Raina, and it wasn't only about lovemaking or the lack thereof. She not only admired Dharr Halim, appreciated his kindness and his concern for her, his comforting embrace. She was starting to feel so much more.

For someone who had no designs on settling down with a sinfully seductive sheikh, she was certainly doing a good impression of a woman falling in love.

Five

As the plane made its final descent, Dharr did not dare to do anything more than hold Raina close to his side. As badly as he wanted to kiss her, he recognized he had already done too much. She had weakened him to the point that he had almost thrown away all caution.

At least she seemed more relaxed now despite the upcoming landing. Her hands rested in her lap as she stared straight ahead, seemingly lost deep in thought. He missed having her head resting against his shoulder, missed distracting her with his kisses. And he knew that once they returned to Azzril, he would miss much more than that.

The plane landed smoothly and in a matter of moments, they were cleared to leave their seats. In silence, Raina gathered her bag from beneath the bed and slipped the strap over her slender shoulder. Dharr almost asked if he could help her but knew he would be met with a resounding "no."

They walked to the door, still not speaking, until Raina faced him. "I guess this is it," she said.

Dharr slipped his hands in his pockets to keep from touching her. "Yes, it seems it is."

"We'll just pretend none of this ever happened."

"We will keep it our secret."

"What about your staff?" She glanced at the bed now in total disarray. "They're going to know something when they change the sheets."

"I trust they will remain silent. They are very loyal to me."

"That's good to know." She worked her bottom lip between her teeth several times before finally looking at him again. "Thanks, Dharr. I would never have made it through my return to flying without you."

"It has been my pleasure." The greatest of pleasures for Dharr. She turned to the door. "I guess we should probably go now."

Before she could release the latch, Dharr rested his hands on her shoulders. "Wait."

After turning her around, he met her soft gold gaze, wariness in her eyes. "What is it?" she asked.

"One more kiss."

"I'm not sure we should."

He brought her hands to rest against his chest. "Only one, to seal our vow of secrecy."

"Okay. Just a little one."

"Of course."

Yet when he bent his head and touched his mouth to hers, as always she opened to him. Her lips were soft, pliant, welcoming. She drew his tongue into the heat of her mouth with gentle persuasion. They wrapped their arms around each other in a tight embrace, feeding each other, feasting on each other.

In another place, at another time, Dharr would notify the crew they would not be leaving soon. He would take her back to the bed and make love to her. Truly make love to her. But in one coherent moment, he realized that would not be possible.

With effort he pulled away from her lips yet kept his arms around her. "That should be sufficient."

Her ensuing smile was shaky. "And you have no concept of 'little.' But that's okay. At least it was memorable."

And so had been their time together, Dharr decided. He longed for more time with her, more touches, more talk. More of everything.

Aside from avoiding her completely while she was in his home, he was uncertain of how he could fight his attraction to her. But he knew he must, or risk certain emotional peril when she left him.

The city had changed, Raina thought as the armored sedan arrived at the highest point of the mountain road revealing, Tomar—the capital city—spread out in the valley below. Amber lights dotted the panorama, providing a breathtaking view. The ancient palace, situated at the gateway to the old village, remained the focal point. But a few high-rise buildings silhouetted against the night sky were scattered on the opposite end of town.

"Tomar's grown quite a bit," she told Dharr who had kept a fairly wide berth between them, physically and emotionally.

"Yes, it has. We have become much more modern."

Raina couldn't argue that point, nor could she argue she wasn't attuned to Dharr's every move, his scent and the taste of him still lingering on her lips.

Rolling down the window, she let the cool desert breeze blow across her face to try and erase all those little details, but to no avail. She could still feel his hands and his mouth on her skin, as if she were completely bared to him.

The vehicle bumped down the barely paved road, jolting

Raina against Dharr's shoulder. She should probably move away from him so as not to create any suspicion, but she found comfort in his touch, even if it was only minor. He didn't reach for her hand as he had on the plane, didn't tip her head against his shoulder, didn't even look as if he wanted to touch her. He continued to stare out the opposite window, totally detached.

Raina decided she might as well get used to it now, the physical and emotional distance. Dharr obviously was more than willing to uphold his hands-off promise. And that made Raina surprisingly disappointed and a little bit peeved.

She'd been nothing more than a readily available diversion. An easy means to pass the time. She meant nothing more to him than that, and she might as well accept it. But isn't that what she'd wanted, too? Yes, and she needed to remember that. She also needed to remember something else. "Could you remind me to call my mother in the morning?"

"That has already been done."

Raina didn't even try to hide her shock even though Dharr still refused to look at her. "You called her?"

"My assistant did, at my request, when we were grounded in London. I felt it best she not worry."

"Don't you think I should have been the one to tell her?"

Finally he glanced at her. "I thought it might be best coming from someone else."

"What exactly did your assistant say to her?"

"That I was escorting you to Azzril to see your father, and nothing more. In fact, he did not speak to her personally but he did reach a woman named Mona who promised to pass along the information."

Mona, the meddling maid. "I'm sure she was very thrilled to do that. I still think I should have called her personally."

"You can call her tomorrow."

Raina could but now that her mother knew exactly where she was, and with whom, it might be best to wait a day or two for her to calm down.

When they pulled up at the palace a few moments later, Raina couldn't get out of the vehicle quick enough, waving off the driver's offer of assistance with her lone bag. She didn't need his help, and she didn't need Dharr Halim.

The doors opened wide as they entered the ornate palace foyer—midnight blue tile with a white border, beige brick walls, black and white mosaic ceiling, two metal Egyptian sentries guarding the wide arched entry showcasing six white-marble stairs with a red-carpeted runner. And at the top of those stairs stood a lone woman dressed in dark clothing, small in stature with a big smile. Raina immediately recognized the endearing features, the salt-and-pepper low bun, the warm and welcoming expression of Badya, Raina's one-time nanny and faithful family employee.

"Welcome home, little one." Badya opened her arms to Raina who gladly accepted her embrace.

"It's so good to see you, Badya," she said after they parted. "What are you doing here?"

"Your father released most of his staff after you left."

The first round of surprising news and, Raina suspected, not the last. "I can't believe he would let you go."

Badya nodded toward Dharr who now stood beside Raina. "The royal family was kind enough to offer me a position as the house manager. I have enjoyed my time here very much although they do not work me very hard."

"She is too modest," Dharr said. "This household would fall down around our heads were it not for her."

"What else am I to do since there are no babies to tend?"

Raina smiled. "You certainly tended to me well, although I did manage to cause you more than a little trouble at times."

"No more than I could manage, *yáahil*." Badya glanced at Dharr then lowered her eyes. "Forgive me. I should refer to you as Princess Kahlil now that you are no longer my charge."

Raina's mouth dropped open before she laughed. "I'm no princess, Badya. I'm just me, the *bint* who used to hang out with you in the kitchen, giving you lots of daily grief."

"Badya is correct," Dharr stated. "You are technically a princess while you are here."

Raina ventured a quick look his way. "But my father was exiled from Fareesa years ago."

"He is still a sultan, and you are still royalty."

"Half royalty," Raina corrected before she turned her attention back to Badya. "How is my father?"

"He is waiting for you," Badya said. "He insisted he would not sleep until he knew you were safe in Azzril."

Raina wanted to see him badly. But she wasn't sure she had the strength to endure any questions about Dharr should he decide to pose them, and she knew he would. "It's the middle of the night. Maybe I should wait until morning."

"He will not stand for that," Badya said firmly, then more quietly, "He has missed you very much and he will not retire until he has spoken with you."

"I will go with you," Dharr said. "Then we will retire to bed."

That sounded like a plan to Raina though she realized he'd meant separate beds. "After you," she said with a sweeping gesture toward the curving staircase leading to the upper floors.

Raina followed Dharr up the stairs, reminding her of two nights ago when she'd done the same in the plane. Only now she knew exactly what his butt looked like without the benefit of slacks.

Once they reached the corridor outside her father's suite,

Dharr turned to her. "If he asks questions about our trip, be brief."

"I know that, Dharr. If we're lucky, this visit will be brief."

"I would not count on it. He has not seen you in a while."

"I'll handle everything fine. You don't have to stay."

"I would prefer to see how he is doing."

The concern in Dharr's tone prompted Raina's latent fears. "Are you not telling me everything? Is he worse than you've been letting on?"

"I have told you everything. I am more concerned with you."

She folded her arms across her chest. "Oh, so you're worried I'm going to spill the beans and tell him we spent a good deal of time fooling around?"

"No. I am concerned that he might press you about our marriage arrangement. I do not want you to have to answer to that alone."

"How chivalrous of you. But again, I know how to handle my own father."

"I am certain you do. I am still going in with you."

Resigned Dharr wasn't going to give up, Raina rapped on the heavy door and waited for her father's "Come in," before she turned the knob.

She stepped inside to find her beloved papa lying on crisp white sheets contrasting with his navy pajamas, his head propped on two pillows, a book resting on his chest and his reading glasses and near-gray hair askew.

Raina propped her hands on her hips and looked mock-disapproving. "Now what are you doing up this time of night, oh stubborn sultan?"

He grinned and held out his arms. "You are here, safe and sound, my child."

"Yes, I'm definitely here."

"Come and let your old papa get a better look at you."

On sluggish legs, Raina walked to him, perched on the edge of the bed and gave him a lengthy hug. "You're not old, Papa. You'll never be old."

He slid his glasses to the top of his head. "I would like to believe that but I fear my physical condition is saying otherwise." When Raina straightened, her father turned his attention to Dharr who was standing near the door. "My thanks to the *shayx* for bringing my daughter to me."

Dharr nodded in response. "It was my pleasure to serve you, Sultan."

Raina laid a hand on his arm. "How are you really feeling?"

He scowled. "Well enough not to be in this bed. I am still in control of all my faculties." He leaned forward and sniffed. "What is that perfume you are wearing?"

Perfume? She didn't have on any perfume. Unless… The oil. And she just thought she'd washed it all off. "It's new. A nice floral scent, don't you think?"

"Ah, flowers. That suits my *záhra.*"

"You're too kind, Papa, but I'm not a flower tonight. I am about to wilt."

He brushed a hand over her cheek. "You do look tired. Did you not sleep on the plane?"

Not hardly. "Yes, I did. Dharr was kind enough to provide his quarters for the duration."

He shot a quick glance at Dharr. "As best I can recall, only one bed exists."

Uh, oh. "Yes. I slept there. Dharr stayed up most of the trip." And that part wasn't a lie.

"Then you two have gotten to know each other better?"

A tremendous understatement. "Yes."

Again her father looked to Dharr. "Would you mind if I spoke to my daughter privately?"

Raina glanced over her shoulder to see Dharr nod. "I will

be outside when you are ready to retire to your room, Raina. Peace be upon you, Sultan."

"And peace be upon you, Sheikh Halim."

After Dharr left the room, Raina turned to find her father's face forming a mask of concern. "Is there something you wish to tell me, Raina?"

She balled her hands into tight fists in her lap. "Tell you?"

"Yes. I feel as if you are concealing something from me."

Darn his intuition. "I'm not, Papa. Everything is going well with work. My life is in order. I'm settling into my new—"

"I am referring to your relationship with Dharr."

Despite internal panic, Raina attempted a relaxed façade. "I promise you, we got along just fine. He's a very interesting man."

"And he treated you well?"

"Of course. Why would you think otherwise?"

"Because you are a beautiful woman and he is a hot-blooded male. And although I consider Dharr the closest thing to a son, if I discover that he treated you inappropriately, I would have to kill him."

Raina released a nervous laugh. "You have a grand imagination, Papa, as always."

"My only concern is for you. I expect Dharr to treat you with the greatest respect and withhold any serious affection, at least until you are married."

Here we go again. "I am not even going to discuss that marriage contract, Papa, because as I've told you before, I have no intention of going through with it."

"You should not be so quick to toss the idea away."

"I don't want to get married right now."

He looked hopeful. "But you have not completely ruled out the possibility in the future?"

Leaning over to kiss his cheek, she told him, "Good

night, Papa. I'm too tired to hash this out now, and you need your rest."

"I am fine." He laid a hand on his chest, contradicting his assertion.

"Are you okay?" Raina asked, her tone laced with worry.

"Again, I am fine. I am taking enough medications to make the most ill of men miraculously recover from any maladies."

"Are you sure?"

He patted her cheek. "I am sure. Now run along to bed. We will talk again tomorrow."

"Okay." Raina saw escape at hand when she reached the door until her father called her back. She faced him once more. "What is it now, Papa?"

"How is your mother?"

Raina's heart clutched when she saw the familiar sadness in his eyes. "She's doing okay. She's not very happy that I moved out."

"She is lonely. How well I understand that."

"It doesn't have to be that way for either one of you, if you'd both quit being so stubborn and admit you still have feelings for each other."

"It is too late for us to be happy," he said. "But it is not too late for you. Search long and hard for that happiness, my daughter. And once you find it, do not let it go."

"I'm happy with my life, Papa." Oddly she didn't sound all that convincing. And her father wasn't convinced. She could see it in his eyes.

"Now get some rest," she said. "I'll see you in the morning."

"I hope so," he murmured. "I would also like to see a grandchild before I pass on to the great unknown."

Without responding, Raina sent him a smile before she rushed out the door.

Dharr was leaning back against the opposite wall of the

corridor, arms folded across his broad chest, looking gorgeous despite his ruffled hair and rumpled shirt. "Shall I show you to your room now?"

"Yes. We need to talk."

Dharr led Raina down the hallway to a room three doors from her father's suite. After they entered the room, she was vaguely aware of the recessed U-shaped sofa beneath an arched overhang and the rich russet colors mixed with turquoise. But she was very aware of the four-poster, carved bed not far away, and that had nothing to do with her lack of sleep.

First and foremost, she had to tell Dharr about her conversation. "Close the door," she said, her tone more anxious than she would have liked.

"Perhaps that would not be a good idea."

"I don't want anyone to hear us."

"Hear us?"

She let go a frustrated sigh. "Talking, Dharr. I think you need to know what my father just said to me."

"As you wish." He closed the door then faced her again. "I am ready to listen now."

Raina wasn't certain how she should tell him, so she simply blurted, "He knows."

Dharr took a few steps forward. "Knows what?"

"He knows that something went on between us."

"How would he know this unless you told him?"

"I didn't say anything that even remotely hinted at our...you know."

"Extracurricular activities?"

She pointed. "Exactly. He obviously sensed something. Maybe it's the oil. He smelled it, you know. I swear I thought I washed it all off—"

"Raina."

"Obviously I didn't, not that I didn't try. But then it was on the sheets when—"

"Raina."

"This morning, when we went at it again. I knew I should have taken another shower—"

He clasped her shoulders, ending her senseless rambling. "He would have no way of knowing it was massage oil. Now precisely what did he say to you?"

"He said that if he learned that you were inappropriate with me, or something like that, he would kill you."

Dharr had the nerve to laugh. "He must be feeling better."

"He said you weren't allowed to touch me intimately."

He dropped his hands from her shoulders. "I see."

"Until we're married."

Any sign of humor disappeared from Dharr's expression. "Then he brought up the marriage arrangement."

"Yes, he did. And I refused to discuss it with him. Of course, he added a little drama by clutching his chest although he insists it's nothing. I'm beginning to believe he might be partially right. Until that point, he looked perfectly fine."

"Do you believe he is manipulating you with his illness?"

Raina wrung her hands over and over. "I honestly believe he probably has been sick. I also believe that now that I'm here, he's going to milk it for what it's worth, hoping to convince me to hook up with you permanently. That was apparent when he mentioned grandchildren."

Dharr paced the length of the room then back again. "All the more reason not to give him anything to be suspicious about."

"I know. It's probably best we don't even look at each other when we're together."

Dharr stopped and frowned. "That would seem rather unusual, do you not agree?"

"Probably so." She shrugged. "I'm sure everything will be fine. Regardless of what he believes might have happened between us, he has no proof. And he did say he considers you the son he never had."

"I am flattered."

"I suppose you should be, although considering what we've done, that seems a little incestuous."

Once more Dharr moved in closer to her. "I assure you that any thoughts I have entertained about you have not been brotherly."

Drawn in by his sultry expression and his mysterious eyes, Raina slipped her arms around his waist. "I would have to say the same about you. I've never thought of you as my brother."

"Raina, we should not be doing this," he said, yet he pulled her totally against him.

"We're not doing anything. It's just an innocent embrace between surrogate family members."

"What I am considering now would not be deemed innocent."

She gave him a coy look. "And what would that be?"

He responded by claiming her mouth in a not-at-all innocent kiss. It was hot. It was deep. It was intoxicating.

But after too short a while, in Raina's opinion, it ended. Dharr stepped back and clamped his hands behind his neck. "You need to sleep."

She needed him. Raina called herself the worst kind of fool—a woman too weak to resist a man who shouldn't interest her at all. But he did. Too much. "You're right. Now run along to your bedroom. By the way, where is your bedroom?"

He dropped his arms to his sides. "You are standing in it."

"You mean we're going to sleep in the same bed again?" She couldn't conceal the surprise, or the excitement, in her voice.

"No. I am taking the suite at the end of the hall. It is smaller than this one and smells of fresh paint. You will be more comfortable here."

Not without him in her bed, as badly as she hated to admit it. "I really don't think it's necessary to put you out of your room. I can take the smaller one. I'm used to the smell of paint."

"I insist. And this room is also closer to your father."

Raina wasn't so sure that was a good thing, especially if in some uncontrolled fit of lust, she might hold Dharr prisoner, bound with some well-placed bed sheets. "If you're sure."

"I am only sure of one thing, Raina." He reached out and touched her cheek. "I will miss not having you in my arms tonight."

With that, he headed out the door without further comment, leaving Raina alone with a total loss of composure.

Unless Dharr Halim took a sabbatical on the other side of the world, for Raina Kahlil, ignoring him would be impossible.

"Will you be escorting Miss Kahlil to the celebration tonight?"

Dharr looked up from the financial documents to Abid Raneer, standing before Dharr's desk, confused over the query. "What celebration?"

"The one commemorating the recent marriage of Ali Gebwa's daughter. Have you forgotten?"

Dharr tossed aside the papers and dashed a hand over his jaw. "Yes, I had forgotten. I suppose I should make an appearance considering he is a major investor in the museum project."

"And one of your father's loyal supporters."

"True."

"You did not answer my original question. Will you be taking Miss Kahlil?"

Dharr had not considered taking Raina to a public function. Yet if he did not, that would be considered inhospitable. "I will ask if she would like to attend."

"Very good, Sheikh Halim. I will inform the sultan since he has been inquiring."

Dharr should have suspected as much. "Does the sultan plan to leave his bed to attend?"

"No. He suggested his daughter go in his stead."

"Again, I will ask." Dharr leaned back in his chair. "Now tell me again what the sultan's wife said when she contacted you after receiving the message?"

"She told me to tell the princess not to do anything she might regret."

"And she gave no other indication as to what that means?"

"I presume it could have to do with you."

Dharr presumed the same and he hoped he did not live to regret what he and Raina had done. "Perhaps she is concerned that the princess might decide to remain in Azzril with her father."

"That could be true, but I'm certain she will not be the only one to speculate on your relationship with Princess Kahlil."

"I do not plan to give anyone any cause for speculation."

"I am afraid you already have."

Concern sat like a massive weight on Dharr's chest. "What do you mean?"

Raneer took the seat opposite Dharr and leaned forward. "Most of your men are loyal to you, but they are still men, and men do talk. I have heard some rumors about your journey with Miss Kahlil."

"Unfounded rumors." Dharr recognized he sounded too defensive, which made him appear guilty. In truth, he was.

"That quite possibly is true, but tonight with you serving as her escort, many will believe you have decided to take her as your bride in accordance with the betrothal."

"Then they would assume wrong. Neither I nor the princess have any intention of upholding the marriage contract."

"Should anyone ask, what do you wish me to say?"

"Simple. The palace has no comment on the sheikh's personal affairs, and leave it at that."

"I believe your father would object to that response."

Anger and lack of sleep began to take its toll on Dharr. "My father is not present and he has left me in charge, so I will handle matters as I see fit. Is that understood?"

As usual, Raneer looked unaffected by Dharr's show of temper. "That is quite clear."

A change of subject was definitely called for, Dharr decided. "Speaking of the king, have you heard from him or my mother?"

"They left implicit instructions that they not be disturbed once they boarded the yacht two weeks ago."

"I suppose that is to be expected since it is their anniversary trip." Even after forty years of marriage, his parents still acted as if they were newlyweds. Yet they had an abiding love for each other, something Dharr had found very rare in his experience. Something he dared not hope for.

Raneer stood. "Is that all, your grace?"

Dharr picked up the documents and pretended to study them once more. "Yes. I have work to do. Tell Badya to inform the princess of our evening outing. If she agrees to attend, then I expect her to be ready no later than 7 p.m. as I do not plan to stay long into the evening."

"I will."

Dharr sensed Raneer staring at him so he looked up. "Is there something else you require, Abid?"

"No. I would only like to say that the princess is a beautiful woman. A man could do much, much worse."

Dharr did not need the commentary, even if Raneer was his

closest aid. "Yes, she is beautiful, and she is a free spirit. Any man who would be foolish enough to fall for her would have to be willing to do things her way."

"Much like yourself, I see."

"You may go now," Dharr said through clenched teeth.

Raneer nodded. "As you wish."

When Dharr was again alone, he tipped his head back against the chair and closed his eyes, the image of Raina arriving with great clarity.

Yes, she was a free spirit, intelligent and full of life. Yes, she would make a man a fine wife—if the man was strong enough to hold her. Dharr did not consider himself to be that man for he had already failed once with another woman who was much the same.

Regardless, the fantasy of making love to Raina took flight again. Now if only he could leave it at that. Yet he admitted that he craved to have the beauty in his arms—in his bed— once more.

Six

She looked like the scruffy side of a camel's hump.

Raina stood before the mirror examining the bags beneath her eyes, all the while thinking she could not believe she'd slept until 5 p.m.

When the knock came at the door, her heart skipped several beats. She started to reach for her robe to cover herself in case it was Dharr, then reconsidered. What the heck? He'd definitely seen her in a whole lot less.

She strolled to the door, her pulse fluttering with excitement and anticipation, only to find Badya on the other side.

"I see you have finally awakened," Badya said as she hurried into the room carrying a tray full of food that she placed on the table in the corner.

"You should've gotten me up hours ago."

"I tried but I could not rouse you."

"You must not have tried very hard."

Badya brought out her familiar grimace, the one she'd always used on Raina when she wasn't too pleased. "I put away all your clothes and still you did not move. I then checked to see if you were breathing, which you were, so I assumed you needed your rest after the flight." She gestured toward the fare. "Now come have something to eat."

Raina walked to the table and wrinkled her nose, her stomach roiling in protest. "I'm not really all that hungry, but I will have some coffee."

After Badya poured her a cup, Raina took a sip and tasted cardamom, bringing back a host of memories from a long-ago time. "I'd forgotten how good this is," she said as she dropped down in one less-than-comfortable chair.

"You really should eat, *yáahil.* You need your strength."

Raina needed strength, all right. At least enough to keep her hands off Dharr. She bypassed the pungent stew and grabbed a pastry that melted like sugar in her mouth. "I remember these date bars, too," she said after she swallowed. "You're still the best cook in Azzril."

"You are kind, *yáahil,* but I no longer cook. It is my recipe, though."

Badya took the chair across from Raina and smiled. "So have you found Sheikh Halim to your liking?"

Raina nearly choked on the cookie. "If you mean do I think he's nice, he's okay."

"I would say by the way that you look at him, he would be more than that to you."

Raina reminded herself to stop eating until this conversation ended. "What do you mean?"

"Perhaps I should say the way you look at each other, as if you share a secret. Perhaps you are in love with him."

Raina rolled her tired eyes and even that took effort. "That's ridiculous. Why would you even think such a thing?"

"Because every woman in this country below the age of sixty is in love with him. You will see that tonight when he escorts you into the village for the celebration."

"What celebration?"

"Two days ago, your childhood friend, Fahra Gebwa married Gameel Attar. Though the couple has left for their wedding trip, the celebration continues."

Wonderful. Fahra had always been a little sneaky snob and Gameel, whose name meant "handsome" in Arabic, was about as attractive—inside and out—as a dried-up blowfish. Like she was really one to talk at the moment. "That's good. She can spend all his money while he establishes his very own harem."

"True, it is not a love match, but a solid match."

"I just pity the children."

Badya laughed. "You are as quarrelsome as always."

Raina stood and stretched. "Only when it comes to people I don't care for."

"And of course, the sheikh would not be among those people."

Was she being that obvious? If so, she needed to practice camouflaging her attraction to Dharr, and fast. She wasn't certain how well she could manage that in the near future, especially in a public forum. "I still don't want to attend the celebration. Besides, I need to visit with Papa."

"It is your father who has ordained it. You are to go in his place."

Great. Just great. First Papa wanted to kill Dharr and now he was throwing him into her path. "I don't have anything appropriate to wear."

Badya came to her feet, strode to the closet and pulled out a teal sleeveless top with beads dangling at the hem and the matching wraparound skirt. "This will do. I will bring you a

Play the

Lucky Hearts *Game*

and get...

2 FREE BOOKS
and a FREE MYSTERY GIFT...

yes! YOURS to KEEP!

I have scratched off the silver card. Please send me my *2 FREE BOOKS* and *FREE mystery GIFT*. I understand that I am under no obligation to purchase any books as explained on the back of this card.

Scratch Here!

then look below to see what your cards get you... 2 Free Books & a Free Mystery Gift!

326 SDL D34S   225 SDL D349

FIRST NAME   LAST NAME

ADDRESS

APT.#   CITY

STATE/PROV.   ZIP/POSTAL CODE   (S-D-10/04)

Twenty-one gets you
2 FREE BOOKS
and a *FREE MYSTERY GIFT!*

Twenty gets you
2 FREE BOOKS!

Nineteen gets you
1 FREE BOOK!

TRY AGAIN!

The Silhouette Reader Service™ — Here's how it works:

BUSINESS REPLY MAIL
FIRST-CLASS MAIL   PERMIT NO. 717-003   BUFFALO, NY

POSTAGE WILL BE PAID BY ADDRESSEE

SILHOUETTE READER SERVICE
3010 WALDEN AVE
PO BOX 1867
BUFFALO NY 14240-9952

NO POSTAGE
NECESSARY
IF MAILED
IN THE
UNITED STATES

shawl to cover yourself since the desert nights can be cool. Now go and bathe and I will help you ready yourself. You need to be downstairs by seven."

Raina grasped for the final excuse. "I need to wash my hair and it won't be dry by then."

"I will braid it as I did when you were a child."

So much for that protest. As usual, Badya had an answer for everything. "Fine, but I doubt I'm going to have any fun."

Badya sent her a wily grin. "I would think a certain prince would have something to say about that."

Dharr was uncertain what to say to the sultan when he answered his summons. He was, however, pleased to find that Idris was seated for the first time since his arrival at the palace from the hospital. "It is good to see you up and about, Idris."

The sultan answered with a smile. "Having my daughter home has renewed my strength." He indicated the settee near the chair, which he now occupied. "Come sit with me a while before you go."

After Dharr complied, he braced for a serious conversation, and he was not disappointed when Idris said, "My daughter is a jewel, and she will be treated as such. Am I clear on this point?"

Hiding his guilt behind a stern expression, Dharr replied, "I am wounded you do not trust me."

"I am a man, Dharr. And I know it is not easy to resist a beautiful woman such as my daughter."

How well Dharr knew that. "You may count on me to treat her with the greatest respect."

"Good. Now have you given any consideration to the betrothal?"

As suspected, Idris was stilling holding out hope that Dharr would marry his daughter. "Raina and I have not discussed that at length, although I do know she plans to return to the States in a few days."

"Then you must prevent her from doing so."

A feat Dharr dare not attempt to undertake. "She is her own person and free to do as she pleases. I would not impose any sanctions on her because of an agreement you made with my father years ago."

"A good agreement, I might add." Although his tone was somber, it was not all that severe.

"These are different times, Idris. We do not hold the same beliefs as your generation."

"And those former beliefs are not always unwise. Marriages agreed upon by arrangement are most always successful. Those brought about by emotions such as love at times do not survive."

Dharr's own words to Raina two days ago. Yet somehow they sounded callous and hollow coming from her father's mouth. "I suppose you are right, but again, we have not broached the subject."

Idris leaned forward and leveled a stern gaze on him. "You should, and soon. My daughter might surprise you."

As far as Dharr was concerned, she already had surprised him at every turn, yet that had nothing to do with the marriage they both adamantly opposed. Still, he would give Idris some hope to avoid any upset. "I will consider it."

At least the sultan looked pleased, even if Dharr had no plan to bring up the contract to Raina again. "Good. Give the Gabwa's my best this evening. And take care with my Raina."

The door creaked open and a soft feminine voice said, "Did someone call me?"

Dharr immediately stood and faced the entry, unprepared for the sight of Raina dressed in an aqua blouse and skirt, her hair pulled away from her forehead and plaited in a long braid, revealing her exquisite features.

"Papa, are you sure you should be sitting up?" she asked as she bypassed Dharr, bringing with her the citrus scent he had detected during their first encounter in California.

"I am quite capable of sitting," Idris said, followed by a grumble.

Raina did not try to conceal her concern. "As long as the doctor says it's okay, I guess it's okay."

Idris's features softened as he looked upon his only child. "You are worried for naught. The doctor says it would be good for me to move around for short periods of time."

When Raina leaned over to embrace her father, Dharr caught a glimpse of bare flesh at her back and the top of the lamp tattoo. He would most certainly be engaged in a battle not to touch her tonight—a battle that would not be easily won.

Raina straightened and frowned. "Are you sure you want me to go into the village? I mean, I just got here."

"Yes, you should go," Idris said. "You need to recapture what is good about this country."

"I know what's good, Papa. I still remember."

"And tonight you shall make more good memories." He sent her a smile and sighed. "You are truly a beauty. You look so very much like your mother."

Dharr could not agree more, even when Raina's frown deepened and she said, "Minus the blond hair and blue eyes."

Idris turned his attention to Dharr. "Is she not beautiful, Sheikh Halim?"

"Yes, she is." More beautiful to behold that most of the women Dharr had kept in his company in the past. "And we are late. The guards are waiting for us and the car is ready."

"Guards?" Raina said, disapproval in her tone.

Idris patted her hand that now rested on the edge of the

table. "You are with a future king, Raina. And though we live in a peaceful country, there are those who would like to see him fall."

Dharr felt as if he had already fallen, down the side of a sheer cliff, grasping for a hold on his emotions every time he looked at Raina.

Raina sent Dharr a quick glance before regarding her father again. "Okay, I guess we should go. Try to get some rest, Papa."

"All I do is rest, my child."

"And you should. Dharr and I will check on you when we return." She turned her head and gave Dharr her smile." It shouldn't be too late, right?"

If Dharr had his wish, their time together would take all night—in his bed. "We shall make it a short evening."

Idris waved a hand in dismissal. "Now run along, young people. Do not give me another thought. I will be soundly sleeping upon your return. Enjoy your evening together."

The sultan's emphasis on the word "together" was not lost on Dharr, and he doubted it would be on Raina, as well. Oddly, Idris kept sending Dharr veiled warnings about his treatment of Raina, yet he seemed determined to keep them together.

Dharr followed Raina to the door and when she turned the knob, he placed his palm on her back as if it were only natural. After dropping his hand, he risked a glance back at the sultan, expecting to find anger in the man's expression. Instead Idris sent Dharr a knowing smile.

Fortunately Idris Kahlil had no knowledge of how thoroughly Dharr had previously touched his daughter. No doubt, he saw through Dharr's carefully formulated façade, and he wondered if tonight, everyone else would, too. Including Raina Kahlil.

Raina was touched by Dharr's attentiveness as he took her hand and helped her from the black sedan parked on the outskirts of the ongoing celebration. At the end of the village proper, modern melded with ancient in the form of multilevel buildings—the core of the business district. She chose to ignore that aspect and concentrate on the place she'd always loved—the true heart of Tomar, rich in history that seemed to be suspended in time, even tonight.

Raina's memories of Azzril had been of a haven for tourists from various countries looking to experience Arabian culture. A Mecca for all peoples and religions. Under Dharr's father's reign, and his father's father before him, they had known for the most part peaceful coexistence within the boundaries, shielded and sheltered from the rest of the world by a range of mountains. Considering the current state of the world, she wondered how long that would continue to hold true. She prayed it did.

The path they now walked had been cordoned off for their arrival, the outskirts surrounded by countless guards. The piquant smell of native foods wafted over the area—most likely *arusia*, the favorite rice dish for celebrations. The scents brought back Raina's fond recollections of a simpler time, before her parents had gone their separate ways. Only then did she realize how much she had missed the atmosphere, the culture that had been a large part of her formative years.

As Dharr navigated the alley separating two small stone buildings, they came upon a blazing fire surrounded by several men dressed in traditional white *dishdashas,* the turban-like *muzzars* resting atop their heads. They quickly came to their feet and bowed at the waist, their eyes lowered as if Dharr were a god. Raina had to admit with his kaffiyeh secured by the gold and blue band, the flowing white robes also trimmed in gold, he could pass for an ethereal being—an earthbound angel—one with dark, dark eyes and a deadly seductive smile.

Dharr acknowledged the men with a polite greeting and nod before continuing on into the center of activity. The sheikh's presence became known little by little, apparent when several of the onlookers turned toward them, muttering amongst themselves. The men bowed reverently and Raina heard a few nervous giggles coming from a gathering of attractive young women wearing brightly-colored *kandouras*— full length gowns—and elaborate jewelry. As Badya had said, females revered him as much as males respected him. Raina knew him as the man, not the prince. Knew him intimately, as a matter of fact. That thought brought a sudden rise of heat to her face.

As Dharr began to mingle with his subjects, Raina hung back, wondering if somewhere in this crowd another woman, maybe several, might know him just as well. Logically, that was highly doubtful. Any woman granted access to a future king would be carefully screened and discreetly presented to him, a woman who would not be seen among the masses.

Raina couldn't quite wrap her mind around Dharr keeping time with courtesans. Of course, that didn't mean he hadn't met more than a few other prospects during his travels. She wouldn't begin to speculate on what he'd done during his Harvard days. And then there was the matter of *the* woman— maybe even that debutante Elizabeth—who at one time captured his heart and for whatever reason, turned him loose. Even though Dharr still hadn't made that admission, she believed its validity. Why else would he be so jaded when it came to love? Why else hadn't he married long before now?

Still, she couldn't imagine anyone who had earned his love actually releasing him. Obviously there was a story there, one she would probably never know. And worse, she would probably never know how he felt about her. Was it only sex for the sake of sex? Was she only one of many who'd expe-

rienced his skills as a lover only to be discarded later? It truly
didn't matter. In a few days, she would be going home, as soon
as she was assured her father was on his way to recovery.
Home to California and the life she had made. Home, alone.

A round of collective sounds of approval came from the
crowd when Dharr waved away a guard to allow a little girl
into the protective circle. He knelt before the child and smiled,
a softer side of Dharr Halim that Raina had never really witnessed until now.

Not exactly true. If she thought back on the days when
she'd known him as only a family friend, she recalled the
times he had treated her as if she might be special. In one instance, he'd sneaked her a few cookies after her parents had
forbidden her from having them before dinner. He'd given her
a few of his favorite books and had forgiven her when she'd
kicked him in the shin—hard—after he'd tugged on her
braids.

At that time, she had been eight and he sixteen, still a
yucky boy in her opinion, at least back then. Now he was a
man. A striking, enigmatic man.

He would make a great king. An exceptional father. A
wonderful husband. But not to Raina Kahlil. Never her. She
reserved the right to choose a man who could love her back,
and that man wasn't Dharr Halim, even though in some ways
she was beginning to wish it could be so.

She kept her attention focused on Dharr. He now sported a
smile reserved for the angelic child presenting him with a red
paper flower as she whispered something in his ear. Then sud-
denly he looked toward Raina and gave her that same smile,
making her heart plunge to the pebbled path beneath her feet.

Dharr patted the little girl's cheek, straightened and started
toward Raina. With each step he took in her direction, her
pulse quickened in response.

Once he stood before her, he offered the flower. "From an admirer."

She took the paper creation and waved to the child who favored her with a toothy grin. But her attention soon turned to Dharr when he said, "Walk with me," and started up the path past the quaint shops lining the border of the commons area where the festivities continued.

As they strolled along at a leisurely pace, surrounded by a contingent of guards in front and behind them, Dharr spoke to her about the recent progress in modernizing Tomar.

When he told her that an art museum was also in the planning stages, Raina came to a stop and faced him. "I'm surprised you didn't say anything to me earlier," she said.

"I assumed you might not be interested."

Her eyes widened. "How could you say that knowing art is my life?"

"In California," he corrected. "Not in Azzril."

That stung Raina more than a little, but she could understand why he might believe that. "I'm interested in anything having to do with art. Do you already have any commitments in terms of collections?"

"I have my own collection I will donate, except for one particular piece."

When the cool breeze intensified, she tightened the shawl around her shoulders even though she wasn't at all cold. Thanks to Dharr's presence. "A very special piece, I take it?"

"Yes. A Modigliani."

One of her favorites. "Wow. I would love to see it sometime."

He leaned over and although they spoke in English, he lowered his voice and said, "It is hanging in my bedroom, over the fireplace. I am surprised you did not notice it."

She hadn't been coherent enough to notice much of anything in the massive bedroom. "You can show it to me later," she murmured, hoping her suggestive comment had gone unnoticed by the surrounding guards who were keeping a safe distance. Considering the return of the fire in Dharr's eyes, it hadn't been overlooked by him.

They started down the walkway once more, passing a shop where a gold lamp showcased behind glass caught Raina's eye. She stepped into the small store where a gray-bearded man stood behind the counter.

In Arabic, she inquired about the price of the incense burner and the shopkeeper informed her it was pure gold, and very pricey. Resigned that it wouldn't be in her budget, she turned away and nearly ran into Dharr head on.

"Do you want it?" he asked her in a sinfully deep voice.

She wanted him, even more than the lamp. "I can live without it."

"You should not have to live without it if it is what your heart desires."

Without waiting for her response, Dharr stepped up to the counter and requested it be wrapped up for Raina without even asking the price. However, she wasn't sure the man could even answer considering his shocked expression and his apparent need to bow several times to his prince.

Raina tugged on Dharr's sleeve to get his attention. "It's gold and I imagine very expensive."

"I can afford it."

"I know that, but you really don't have to do it."

"I could tell by your eyes that it captured your fancy."

"Maybe I should rub it and see if a genie pops out. Then it might be worth the price."

He leaned over once more and whispered, "I prefer to rub the other lamp you have in your possession."

While Raina fought a strong case of the shivers over the sensual suggestion, Dharr took the package from the man and handed it to her. "It is now yours," he said, then told the shopkeeper to send him the bill personally.

And just like that, Raina was holding a priceless lamp and a desperate longing for the prince who had presented it to her. But as they started away once more, she began to realize the extent of Dharr's true worth when he continued to pause now and then to acknowledge his people, taking careworn hands into his, patting the heads of children, as if he were as common as the rest. In reality, he was quite uncommon to Raina—a man who truly cared about something beyond finding a new way to get a quick rush. A man who didn't take his responsibility lightly.

Dharr stopped and turned his attention to the commons when a drum began to beat, announcing the *Razha,* a celebratory dance performed by men sporting swords and spouting poetry. Raina stood by him and took in the wonderful spectacle she remembered from her youth. The moderate wind continued to blow, but that didn't relieve the heat when Dharr twined his fingers through hers. The gesture surprised her even though he held their joined hands close to his body, the robes providing some measure of concealment.

Several fires dotted the area, illuminating the performers in an almost surreal haze. The strong scent of sandalwood *bokhur* wafted over the area from the incense shop behind them. The drumbeats picked up in tempo as the men began to leap in a frenzied free-for-all.

When Dharr stroked his thumb over her wrist, Raina experienced a bout of dizziness. She felt drunk even though not a drop of alcohol had touched her lips. Totally intoxicated by Dharr's touch alone. If only she could step in front of him, lean back against him, have his arms wrapped around her, then that would make the night almost perfect. Almost. She could think of one other thing that would definitely involve perfection—making love with Dharr.

When Raina swayed toward him, Dharr clasped his arm around her waist and held her to his side. "Are you not feeling well?"

"I'm just a little light-headed." Her voice was so soft he barely heard her.

He told her, "Wait here," took the flower and package from her then approached his most trusted guard. After handing him the items, Dharr voiced his concerns in English so as not to be understood by most of the onlookers, requesting a place he could take Miss Kahlil for a time until he discerned if they would need to leave sooner than planned.

After Dharr made his way back to Raina's side, the guard approached the nearby shopkeeper who gestured toward the back of his store. Again Dharr took Raina's hand and when it appeared no one was looking, he pulled her into the shop's interior.

"Where are we going?" she inquired.

"In here," he said as he opened the door at the end of the aisle, revealing a small storeroom lined with shelves and boxes.

Dharr guided Raina to the only open space and positioned her back against the wall. "This has been too much activity for you. I should have insisted you stay at the palace tonight. You should rest a while, and then we will go."

She sent him a sultry smile. "I'm having a wonderful time."

"You seemed as if you might faint."

"Not at all. I feel fine."

And she looked incredibly beautiful. The fullness of her mouth, the length of her slender neck, the golden glow of her eyes only served to heighten his arousal. She had totally captivated him from the moment she'd entered her father's room, and even more so as he'd witnessed the firelight washing over her when he'd accepted the gift from the child. He was still completely captive to her, yet he was also concerned over her health. "Are you certain you are feeling well enough to continue?"

A long breath drifted from her parted lips. "I admit, I was a little light-headed for a few moments, but I think it was a combination of several things. The fires. The dancers. The incense." She slipped her hands beneath his robes and rested them on his waist. "Being so close to you."

He braced one palm on the wall above her head and kept the other arm at his side to prevent touching her. "This is unwise, Raina."

She exhaled a ragged breath, her gaze trained on his. "I want to be with you again, Dharr. I'm tired of pretending that I don't want you."

So was he. "We have only had to maintain that pretense for less than a day."

"For me, an hour was too long."

"But we said—"

"I know what we said. And if you tell me now—right now—that you don't want me as much as I want you, then I'll keep up the front."

The words would not form in his mouth for if he should speak them, he would be telling a grave untruth. Yet instead of a verbal reply, he professed his absolute need for her with a kiss so deep she would have no doubt. With his hands roving up her back beneath her blouse. With a press of his pelvis against hers to remove any question from her mind as to how much he wanted her.

He slid his palms up her sides then back down to her waist, his knuckles brushing against the sash that with only a tug he could have unbound in a matter of seconds, sending her skirt down her thighs to the cement floor. He could send her underclothes to follow and lower his fly, concealing them with the fullness of his robes, and know how it would feel to finally be inside her.

No one would disturb them. No one would be the wiser.

Yet she deserved better than lovemaking against a pitted wall inside a crowded storeroom. She deserved time to reconsider before it was too late.

When she reached for his fly, Dharr clasped her wrist to halt her. "Again, I have nothing to protect you from pregnancy."

She gave him a beseeching look. "I know this sounds crazy, and maybe I am, but I need to touch you *now,* Dharr. I want you to touch me."

He wanted that more than the respect of his people at the moment. "Not now. Not this time."

"Then you don't want me." Disappointment resounded in her tone.

To reassure her, he kissed her again before saying the only truth he knew at that moment. "This time, I want to be inside you."

Her eyes took on a wildness, exciting Dharr beyond all bounds. "Then do it. Soon."

Dharr said goodbye to his wisdom, or perhaps he had done that the moment Raina had walked onto the plane and back into his life. Yet that no longer mattered. Before she left him, he would have her, as long as he knew she understood exactly what she was asking.

Holding her face in his palms, he studied her eyes, making certain he did not find any hesitation. He did not.

"I promise you, Raina, I will finish this. Tonight."

Yet somehow he knew this would be only the beginning.

Seven

In the darkened sedan, Dharr kept a decent space between them. To Raina, it seemed like a hundred miles, and so had their return to the palace.

He'd remained quiet, not uttering a word on the journey. Of course, she hadn't said anything, either, because for the life of her, she didn't know what to say. She couldn't explain why she *had* to be with him because she didn't understand it herself. But she didn't feel the need to apologize for her behavior because she wasn't at all sorry. At least not yet.

She certainly might be sorry should Dharr change his mind and not follow through on his promise. She was beginning to believe that very thing when he failed to look at her, even when she asked, "How much longer?"

"We are almost to the gates."

"Good. I wondered if maybe we were lost."

"No. We both know exactly where we are going."

Reaching across the seat, Dharr laid her open palm on his thigh, then slowly, slowly, drew it upward until she contacted the unmistakable ridge before he placed her hand back on the seat between them.

A subtle answer to her question, but very much an answer, and one that made her heartbeat increase at an alarming rate.

Moments later, the motorcade entered the massive iron gates and pulled up in front of the palace. Dharr left the sedan first, offering his hand to Raina, which she took without a second thought. She had no second thoughts at all, especially when Dharr stroked his thumb over her palm before releasing her once more.

By the time she walked through the heavy double doors, Raina wanted to sprint up the stairs, shedding her clothes on the way. Not a wonderful idea considering Badya was waiting for them by the black iron banister.

"Did the sheikh and the princess have a good time tonight?" Badya asked in a pleasant voice.

"Most certainly," Dharr said from behind Raina.

"Is my father still awake?" she asked, feeling somewhat guilty when Badya confirmed that he had been asleep for hours and said he would see Raina in the morning.

"I'm off to bed then," Raina said, her tone overly cheerful, something she was sure Badya had noticed.

"Have a restful sleep," Badya replied, giving Raina a subtle cautioning look, confirming her suspicions.

Once she started up the stairs, Raina didn't dare glance back at Dharr or her former nanny. Anticipation, exhilaration, brought heat to her cheeks that traveled down her throat and spiraled throughout her entire body. Not until they reached the bedroom door did she face Dharr.

He looked down the hall both ways, then said, "I will retire to my quarters until the final guard passes."

"But you'll be back?" Raina hated how unsure she sounded, and worse, almost desperate.

"You may depend on it." He took one more quick glance down the hall, leaned forward and grazed his palm down her bottom before brushing a gentle kiss over her lips. "Be waiting for me."

Oh, he didn't have to worry about that, and Raina would have told him so had he not strode away, tearing the kaffiyeh off as he headed to the end of the hall and his room.

Raina waited until he completely disappeared before she entered her own room. His room, actually, and she'd been very aware of that fact when she'd seen his clothes hanging next to hers, smelled his sultry scent in the bath suite, investigated all his colognes and shaving supplies like some silly smitten school girl.

But tonight, the girl wouldn't be present. The woman would, waiting with great eagerness for a man who could answer every one of her fantasies.

Quickly she stripped out of all her clothes, took her hair out of the braid, turned down the lights and sheets, then stretched out on her back to wait for Dharr's arrival. Only minimal illumination filtered into the sheer curtains from the guard lights in the center courtyard. The clock on the far wall ticked down, second by second, minute by minute, while Raina stared at the octagonal recessed ceiling, attempting to count the crisscrossed sky blue tiles overhead though she couldn't really see them well. She turned her attention to the stone fireplace across the room where Dharr's favored painting hung above the mantel. Even the priceless nude couldn't hold her attention for very long.

The waiting, watching, wanting was excruciating and when more time had passed, Raina wondered if Dharr had changed his mind. Then she heard the door open and close, the click of the lock and the footfalls coming nearer and nearer.

She turned her head and saw him standing by the bed, powerful and imposing as he meticulously removed his clothes until she wanted to squirm and tell him to hurry. Once he was completely nude, he tossed something onto the nightstand, condoms Raina assumed. At least tonight he was prepared.

But she wasn't exactly prepared for the rush that went straight to her head when the mattress gave with his weight. He took her into his arms and kissed her thoroughly, gliding his tongue in an erotic tempo that foretold what he would do to her body. After a time, he feathered kisses along her jaw, down her throat and the valley between her breasts before drawing a nipple into his mouth, circling his tongue round and round until Raina thought she might fall into the realm of full-blown insanity. Yet he didn't linger long before he skated his lips down her abdomen, bracing her hips in his large palms as if to hold her completely imprisoned.

Raina couldn't muster much more than a shaky breath, couldn't budge other than to rest her palms on his head. She certainly didn't have enough force to protest, not that she wanted to, even when he kept going until his mouth was firmly planted between her thighs, plying her with the ultimate, intimate kiss.

Such sweet tyranny, such an absolute possession, as if he were marking his territory with his capable mouth. The building pressure coiled tighter with every sweep of his tongue, every tug of his lips. She tried to delay the inevitable, locking her jaw tight while tuning into every wonderful sensation. Higher and higher he took her as he lifted her hips up to gain full advantage, tearing away any plans she had to prolong the experience. She climaxed with a violent shudder, then another until she feared she might never stop shaking.

He worked his lips back up her body to her mouth then kissed her lightly once, twice, before leaving her arms. She wanted to groan in protest until she realized what he was doing after she heard the sound of tearing paper. Still, he kept his palm curled between her thighs, teasing her into another frenzy while he tended to the protection.

Now was probably a good time to tell him he would be her first lover. But if she made the revelation, would he change his mind? He might, and if he did, she would surely die from frustration. For that reason, she opted to go with the flow and explain herself after the fact.

Once again he came back to her, hovered over her and ran his hands through her hair. "I must ask you again," he said, his voice a rough whisper. "Are you certain?"

Now she was truly frustrated. "Dharr, if you stop, I'll scream."

He brushed a kiss over her temple. "I suggest that you might scream before the night ends, but not because I will fail to see this through." He moved over her, dividing her legs with his muscular thigh. "And hopefully not because I cause you too much pain, although you will experience some this first time."

He knew. "I understand that."

"Then you have not been with another man."

Raina realized he'd been baiting her into the admission. "It's okay, Dharr. I want this."

"As do I, but—"

She pressed a fingertip against his lips to silence his concerns. "No more questions. No regrets. We've come this far, we can't turn back. I don't want to turn back."

Just when she thought he might reconsider, he eased into her, carefully, methodically, stretching her to accommodate him. He wasn't a small man by any means and she wasn't sure how she could take all of him, but he saw that she would with one sharp thrust.

Raina tried to muffle the gasp, without success. He stilled

and spoke to her in a voice as soft as the shadows, alternating between English and Arabic, telling her in gentle tones how good she felt surrounding him. How long he had wanted this, wanted her. Lulled by his words, Raina's body relaxed until he began to move inside her with careful strokes. He kissed her again, first her mouth then her breasts, rubbed against her, creating a delicious friction that had her bordering on another orgasm that threatened to match the first. He clasped her bottom, drawing her closer to him and using his fingertips to explore while he maintained a steady cadence. But soon the act took a frenzied turn as he picked up the pace, harder and faster, until Raina clung to his shoulders and without thought, raked her nails down his back.

She surrendered to the rippling climax, hung on to him and rode each surge. Dharr's back went rigid against her palms, his heart pounding against her breast, and an almost feral groan left his lips now resting at her ear. He remained still for a few moments, silent, then muttered a mild oath in Arabic.

"What's wrong?" she asked, hoping it had nothing to do with her, or what they'd just done, but fearing it did.

He rolled away from her and settled her against his side, her head resting on his shoulder. "It was over too quickly."

Raina relaxed with relief. "I'm not sure I could've stood much more."

He tensed. "Did I hurt you that badly?"

She released a soft laugh. "I meant it was almost too good, if you know what I mean."

"I suppose I do."

Now for the question foremost in her mind. "How did you know I'd never been with anyone?"

"I was not certain but I did have a few suspicions. Or perhaps it was only wishful thinking."

She raised her head and frowned at him. "Oh, so it's that 'I'm macho and I want to be the first' thing."

He stroked his fingertips up and down her arm in an enticing rhythm. "You are an extraordinary woman, Raina. I did not want to consider a man taking advantage of you, although I might fall into that category considering I took your virginity."

She playfully slapped at his chest. "Oh, come on, Dharr. It was my choice. My decision as to who and when. And I chose you."

"Why me, Raina?" He looked and sounded much too somber for such a special time.

How could she explain when she could only speculate? "Maybe it's because I knew you would treat me well. Maybe it's because I knew you would know what you're doing. I wanted my first experience to be with someone I trust." Someone she cared about much more than she should.

He touched his lips against her temple. "I hope you were not disappointed."

She rose above him and pushed a lock of dark hair away from his forehead. "Let me tell you how disappointed I was." She kissed his cheek then his lips. "When we can do it again?"

Even in the limited light, his smile knocked her heart for a loop. "You surprise me, Raina. For one so young, you have very strong appetites."

"I'm twenty-five, Dharr, not fifteen. And I've suppressed my appetites longer than most so I have a lot of catching up to do."

His smile disappeared. "After tonight, if we should continue our intimacy, we risk getting caught."

"Maybe that's why it's so exciting."

"Then you are saying you wish to continue this affair until you leave?"

Affair. There it was. The cold hard truth. But wasn't that

exactly what she'd wanted? Of course. Just a few stolen moments with a sexy, mystifying man who had no plans for commitment. Grab whatever time she could have with him, until the time came for her to return to California. And then tell him goodbye for good, even if she would never forget him.

She forced a smile around the sudden ache in her heart. "Well, considering our recent history, I'm not sure we're going to be able to stop. So yes, I don't see why we shouldn't enjoy each other while we have the time."

"We would have to be very discreet."

"I can do discreet." If her face—and heart—didn't give her away.

She planted a kiss on his chest then raised her gaze to him once more. "So do you think we might give it another go in a little while?"

He didn't seem all that responsive to her request, apparent in his guarded expression and his rigid frame. "You and I both need to sleep tonight. It would be best if we do that, in separate beds."

She couldn't stand the thought of him leaving just yet. "Stay a while, Dharr. Just a little while."

He brought her head to rest on his chest and held her tightly. "I suppose I could stay for a time, at least until you fall asleep."

Raina relaxed against him, reveling in his heat, his strength, his embrace. Yet as she closed her eyes, she fought the sudden sting of unexpected tears. This should be the best night of her life, and in many ways it was. But she also knew it would be over too soon, and too few hours remained in Dharr Halim's arms, and his life.

The first light of dawn streaming in from the window brought Dharr completely awake. With Raina securely swathed in his arms, he had fallen into a deep, restful sleep for the first time in months. Yet should anyone learn he was in her bed, the consequences would be great. Especially if her father became privy to that knowledge.

Working his arm from beneath her, Dharr sat on the edge of the feather mattress and forked both hands through his hair. He must leave her soon, yet he could not resist looking at her one more time. She rested on her belly, her face turned toward him, eyes closed. Her hair, crimped because of the braid she'd worn the evening before, flowed down her back in soft waves. The curve of her bottom and the length of her legs only served to heighten his morning arousal. If they were free to do as they pleased, he would make love to her again.

Impossible. He had already dishonored her in many ways by making love with her once. Considering his suspicion, he should have asked again if she'd been with another man, before they had reached the point of no return. He should have stopped even then. He was not that strong in her presence, had not been strong from the beginning.

Coming to his feet, he snatched his clothes from the floor and went into the bathroom to wash, dress and destroy the evidence of their lovemaking. If only he could be so sure that what they had done would not eventually destroy her good standing with her father, or Dharr's resolve to keep his emotions protected. In that regard, he could already be too late, for what he felt for her had begun to take a turn beyond mutual need and desire.

Yet he had little time today to ponder that. He had several meetings scheduled, beginning in only a few hours. For that reason, he took one last glance at Raina and forced himself to leave before he disregarded his duty.

As he walked the hall toward his room, Dharr immediately noticed Abid standing near the doorway, leaning against the wall, holding a newspaper in his hand. Obviously it was much later than Dharr had realized, and much too late to conceal exactly where he had spent the night. No doubt his assistant had seen him leave Raina's quarters. Of course, he could say he'd forgotten something in his room. Or he could say nothing at all since it was not Raneer's concern, and he could trust him not to ask any questions.

"Are you certain spending the evening with Miss Kahlil was wise, your grace?" Abid asked as Dharr approached, shattering all expectations.

Dharr pushed open the door without looking at him. "I had to retrieve something from my room."

"I see."

The suspicion in Abid's tone, though warranted, did not please Dharr. He turned on his assistant and gave him a steely look. "Why you are here so early in the morning?"

Abid offered the newspaper. "I thought you should see this immediately."

Dharr took the paper and understood all too well his assistant's concern when the front-page headline came into view. Yet the accompanying photograph was much more telling—and damning—a picture of the sheikh and the princess standing near the shop where they had taken shelter, his arm around her and her head resting on his shoulder.

For a long moment Dharr stared at the paper in stunned disbelief before leveling his gaze on Abid. "Do you know how this came to be?"

"I presume the press made this assumption from that photograph taken last evening."

Dharr slammed the paper down on the nearby desk. "I ordered you to keep the press away."

"We carried out that order as best we could. That photograph could have been taken by a local or a tourist, then sold for a substantial sum."

"Are we certain no one among the staff is responsible for this?"

"I have no way of knowing for certain."

After pacing the room for a few moments, Dharr walked to the window and stared out over the landscape. The sun had begun to rise on the city, normally his favorite time of day. Yet he dreaded what might come in the following hours.

"What did the article say about the princess?" he asked, keeping his back to Abid.

"Only that she has been living in America."

Dharr turned and faced his attaché again. "Has the sultan seen it?"

"Not as far as I know."

"Good."

"But he is quoted in the article."

"Quoted?"

"You both have his blessing on the union and he hopes you both get to know each other well."

Idris had no idea how well they knew each other, and if he did know, he would no doubt withdraw any blessings. And worse, Raina would soon learn of the news. He could not begin to speculate how she would react. "I would prefer to tell the princess about this myself."

Abid nodded. "I will make certain she comes to you when she awakens. How do you wish to respond?"

Collapsing into the chair near the foot of the bed, Dharr rubbed his unshaven chin. "I will consider that in the next few hours."

"I could demand a retraction."

"That would call more attention to the princess."

"And if we say nothing, more supposition will abound."

How well Dharr knew that to be true, yet he was too exhausted to consider anything other than taking a shower to ready for his day—and how he would break the news to Raina. After she discovered that the entire country, quite possibly many countries, had begun to assume she had returned to marry him, she would want to leave immediately. Even if not, she would probably withdraw from him, and that bothered Dharr on a deeper level than he cared to acknowledge.

"One more thing," Abid said in a serious tone. "I heard from the king this morning."

"And he said?"

"He will be cutting his trip short in order to return the night of the reception for the Doriana diplomats at the end of the week."

"Did he say why?" Dharr asked though he already had his suspicions.

"He mentioned he wanted to be present for the official announcement of your engagement."

Dharr did not bother to inquire how his father was already privy to the news. As it had always been, any information involving his activities traveled at lightning speed.

He stood and indicated the door. "You may go now, Abid. I will see you in the conference room within the hour."

Abid executed a slight bow. "As you wish, your grace." He turned but as he reached the door, faced Dharr again. "You may trust that what I witnessed this morning will go no further."

"I appreciate your loyalty."

Yet Dharr doubted Raina would appreciate any of the recent events, except perhaps what had happened between them last night. At least he hoped that would be the case, because it seemed it would probably be the last time.

Raina realized she didn't look at all different this morning. A flicker of heat radiated from the inside out as she stood in front of the bedroom mirror, combing out her damp hair in long strokes reminiscent of Dharr's touch. She both dreaded and longed to see him again. Dreaded it because she didn't want to find any regret in his eyes. Longed for it because she missed him more than she thought possible.

When the knock came at the door, she fumbled with and flipped the brush onto the dresser with a noisy clatter, nervous anticipation making it impossible to maintain a firm grip on anything, especially her composure. But when she opened the door to Badya again, anticipation turned to frustration.

Badya whisked past her carrying a full tray and sporting a cheery smile. "I have come with your breakfast, *yáahil.*"

The last thing Raina wanted was food even though she should be starving. But what she wanted right now was a little bit of privacy, or a lot more of Dharr.

Raina grabbed up the brush and resumed grooming without looking at Badya. "You're determined to fatten me up while I'm here, aren't you?"

"Yes. That is my job. To tend to your needs, as I have in the past. As soon as I change your linens, I will be out of your way."

Before she could protest, Raina heard Badya's gasp coming from the direction of the bed.

"Oh, Raina. What have you done?"

Raina gripped the brush and closed her eyes. She could imagine exactly what Badya was seeing—the obvious signs of first-time lovemaking marking the sheets, faint but discernible.

"Don't jump to conclusions, Badya. It was just a visit from the monthly curse."

"Or perhaps a visit from the sheikh. I am not a fool, *yáahil.*"

Raina turned to issue another rebuttal, only to find Badya staring at the condom packages on the nightstand. She had no recourse but to tell her former nanny the truth.

She leaned back against the dresser, gripping the robe tightly to her. "It's no big deal, Badya." Lie number one.

"Neither of us planned it." Lie number two. "I doubt it will happen again." Lie number three, or so Raina hoped, even now that she'd been caught.

Badya collapsed into the settee near the window. "It meant nothing more to you than that? Did your mother and I not teach you anything?"

No, but Dharr had. "This doesn't have anything to do with you or my mother. It was my decision, and it's done."

"In my day, you two would be forced to marry after such behavior."

"It is not your day and neither of us intend to marry."

Badya shook her head. "I am very disappointed in the sheikh. He should know better than to take advantage of an innocent."

This time Raina laughed. "I hate to tell you this, but it wasn't all his idea. Your little girl's grown up, Badya. She's a woman now." A woman who happened to be very enamored of a man who was the consummate lover.

"That might be true, but you are still my *bint*."

Raina pushed away from the bureau, walked to Badya, leaned down and hugged her neck. "I'll always be your little girl in a way. And I hope you won't say anything to anyone about this."

Badya laid a hand on her ample breasts. "I would never do such a thing, even though I would greatly like to give the sheikh a good scolding."

"That won't be necessary." Raina suspected he'd already scolded himself quite a bit on this morning after. Funny, she didn't feel like doing any such thing. She had no regrets whatsoever, only some fine memories of a fantastical experience.

After coming to her feet, Badya embraced Raina again. "I have much to do this morning, so I will leave you for now to dress, then return with fresh linens. Unless you require something else of me. Perhaps my advice on the virtue of being virtuous?"

Too late. "That's enough, Badya. It's done and nothing can change that."

Badya shook her head. "Yes, you are right. I only hope you do not suffer from your decision."

Suffering was not an appropriate word to describe Raina's mood. Euphoric would come much closer although she didn't dare tell that to her self-appointed guardian. "I want to see Papa. Is he awake?"

"Yes, but first the sheikh would like a word with you."

"Now?"

"Immediately." Badya gave her a quick once over. "Or at least after you dress appropriately, although I am certain he has seen you in much less."

Obviously the woman wasn't going to let it go. Normally Raina would toss out a blistering retort, but she knew that would be futile under the circumstance. "Did the sheikh say what he wanted with me?"

Badya clucked her tongue while Raina bit hers. "I can only imagine. But he did not say exactly."

"Did he seem at all upset?"

"Yes, and with good cause."

Reaching around Raina, Badya snatched the newspaper from the breakfast tray and held it up. "Congratulations, Princess Kahlil. It seems you are going to be the next queen of Azzril."

Eight

"**T**he Sheikh Claims His *Bride'?* Oh, please."

Dharr glanced up from the museum blueprints to Raina standing in the entry of the conference room, the newspaper clutched in her raised fist. With her hair bound high atop her head, her golden eyes alight with anger, she looked so much like an adult version of the former hellion, he almost smiled. Almost. Though she had greatly matured, he could not trust that she would not attempt to wrestle him to the ground. However appealing that might be at the moment, it would definitely not be appropriate for the seriousness of the situation.

"Close the door," he told her as he stood and rounded the lengthy table.

After she obeyed, Raina strode across the room to stand before him. "Do you have any idea how much trouble this is going to cause us?"

Dharr's current trouble involved recovering enough of his will not to kiss her or release each button on the plain white blouse to touch his lips to the valley of her breasts. "I do not consider it all that troublesome." A small falsehood to assist in alleviating her concerns.

"Are you serious?" She shook out the paper and held it up in his face. "Nice picture, don't you think? And that headline. Priceless. Funny, no one asked me a thing about my *engagement*."

As she turned her back and began to walk the room, Dharr said, "Our betrothal has been common knowledge for many years."

When she spun on him with fury calling out from her eyes, Dharr realized he had said the wrong thing.

"Is that why you really brought me here?" she asked. "Are you plotting with my father to make sure that I uphold our ridiculous arrangement? Maybe that's what last night was all about, deflower the sultan's daughter and then she would have to marry you?"

Dharr tamped down his anger over the accusations, particularly the final one, knowing that her distress was speaking for her. "I assure you, I had nothing to do with this. The media has a way of skewing the truth to suit their insatiable appetite for sensational news. As I've told you before, I have no desire to marry now or in the near future. And in regard to our evening together, I believe that was mutual." As well as unforgettable despite his guilt.

She looked somewhat contrite. "I'm sorry. You're right. At least about last night. But if you didn't leak this information, then who did?"

"It is only speculation due to our appearance together last evening. Those who would wish it to be will believe it."

"My father, for one." She tossed the paper onto the table

behind him. "He thinks a *marriage* between us would be the best thing since the invention of crossword puzzles and electric razors. This will thrill him."

He weighed his options and chose to unveil his own supposition. "Your father could be in part responsible."

"He wouldn't do that," she said with conviction.

"Did you not read the entire article? He has been quoted."

She grabbed the newspaper again and skimmed it silently before saying, "I can't believe he would stoop so low as to use the press to further his own pipe dreams."

"Perhaps he was not entirely responsible, yet he did seem rather pleased to give his blessing."

Once more she tossed the paper aside. "I'm tempted to give him a good piece of my mind."

"I understand, but considering his condition, perhaps it would be best if we simply ignore it."

"And you think it will all go away, just like that?"

Dharr knew better yet he was unsure how to handle the situation to suit everyone involved. "We will neither substantiate nor deny the information. When you return to California, that will serve as confirmation we've chosen not to adhere to the arrangement." And that would be a day he would not necessarily welcome, for many reasons.

Raina rubbed her temples and lowered her eyes. "Maybe that would be the best way to handle it. Just ignore the whole thing and hope it goes away."

She walked to the window and pushed open the curtained doors to reveal the verandah and the view of the street below. "What is going on down there?"

Dharr moved behind her to find hordes of people gathered at the perimeter of the palace. Many were holding up signs of congratulations, a few were laying flowers on the ground at the iron fencing, others chanting Raina's name.

He knew the first signs of notoriety, and soon Raina would, too. "I believe those are your admirers."

She looked back at him. "Mine?"

He rested his hand at her waist, savoring the feel of bare flesh where the top did not quite meet her black slacks. "News travels quickly here. They want to pay homage to the woman they believe could be their future queen."

She turned her attention back to the crowd. "But they're wrong. I'm not queen material."

Dharr could definitely argue that point. "You're beautiful, Raina. The daughter of a sultan. A perfect prospect."

She released a mirthless laugh that died when several villagers began to point toward the window. The sound of applause and gleeful shouts filtered in through the closed doors.

"Oh, wonderful," she said. "They've spotted us."

"Perhaps you should go out and answer their summons."

Once more she regarded him, alarm reflecting in her gaze. "Alone? I can't do that. I'm not like you. I've never faced anything like this."

"I will go with you."

"Won't that put you in danger, out in the open without your guards?"

The only danger at present was his overwhelming craving for her that could not be denied. "I have addressed my people from this very spot. As soon as the guards are made aware, they will position themselves accordingly."

She frowned. "You're really serious about this?"

"Yes. But it is solely your decision."

She shrugged. "Oh, why not. Might be kind of fun at that. I don't want anyone to think I'm a snob."

Dharr reached around her and released the bronze latch to open the door. The moment they stepped out beneath the iron lattice overhang, a roar emanated from the masses, the likes of which he had never known. Resting his palm against her back, he guided Raina to the end of the balcony, leaving a few feet between them and the edge of the railing. The guards immediately formed a protective shield along the sidewalk and streets.

As he watched her reaction, Dharr witnessed Raina's transformation. The sun cast her features in a radiant glow, shadowing the hollows of her cheekbones and highlighting her heart-shaped face. Her soft, pink lips shimmered as she smiled and waved to the crowd, a portrait of eloquence and grace.

Several photographers snapped pictures, but Dharr knew they could not do justice to her splendor—a beauty that started within before rising to the surface.

If she were queen, she would be beloved. Venerated, as his mother had always been. The marked adoration in the faces of his people filled him with pride, as if he actually had a claim on her. As if he planned to have her as his wife, not only as his lover. That could never be. Raina deserved a man who was whole and able to commit his heart as well as his life to her. And he realized all too well she, too, would leave him in pursuit of her own life, even if he thought he could give what she needed.

The crowd began to chant, requesting them to kiss. Raina turned and held him captive with her sensual smile, dared him with her golden eyes. So caught up on the moment, he pressed his lips to hers but only briefly. Yet it proved to be enough to draw more approval from his subjects as well as impact his own composure.

Raina masked her surprise well, at least superficially. "We've really done it now," she said through another bright smile.

"I am only giving them what they want."

"You're leading them to believe that we're really engaged."

"We were definitely engaged last night, even if not in terms of our marriage arrangement. But I do remember being joined in a mutual endeavor that I greatly enjoyed."

She sent him a quelling look before turning back to the crowd. "Stop it or I'm going to jump you right here in front of the masses. Wouldn't that make for a nice front page photo?"

"I would not want to share you with anyone in that regard."

She rested a palm at her throat. "Why, Dharr, you sound almost possessive."

He did, and he not only sounded that way, he felt that way, as well. "As long as you are in my company, I plan to keep you all to myself."

She continued to wave. "Sounds interesting. Can we go back inside now?"

"Certainly."

After a final acknowledgment of his people, Dharr gestured toward the door and followed Raina inside. Once there, the underlying tension hung thick over them while they stood face to face in the middle of the room. As Raina walked into his arms, he claimed her supple mouth in another kiss. This time their joining could not be deemed innocent or brief. As always, they feasted on each other, hands roving over each other's backs and hips, until they were both winded and forced to draw a breath. They only parted for a short while until they resumed the kiss, deeper this time, more ardent.

Dharr spun Raina around and backed her against the wall, forming his body to hers so she would know how much he wanted her. She answered with a tremor as he worked the buttons on her blouse, parting it enough to slide his mouth down her neck to the rise of her breasts.

He lifted his head and sought her eyes. "I need to be here," he murmured as he pressed his palm between her thighs. "But not now. Tonight."

She gave him a pleading look. "I can't wait until tonight. I'll go nuts."

Dharr had already sufficiently arrived in that state of madness that he'd experienced in her presence more than once. It only worsened when Raina lowered her eyes and lowered the zipper on his slacks.

This could not be, he told himself over and over as she freed him, playing her fingertips over him until he relinquished all his control. He pulled the drawstring at her waist and shoved her pants down to her thighs then did the same to his own. Balanced on the brink of taking her right there, without regard to the consequences, a knock sounded at the door, forcing them apart.

"What do you want!" Dharr shouted as he fumbled to redo his fly while Raina swiftly readjusted her own clothing.

"I have a message for the princess, your grace."

Abid. His timing had been both bad and good. Bad because Dharr wanted Raina with a need so great he would again throw all caution aside. Good because the interruption had prevented that very thing.

"Come in" Dharr answered in a tone that indicated his frustration.

"Excuse me, your grace," Abid said as he stepped into the room, keeping his eyes lowered as if he knew exactly what he had interrupted. "Princess Kahlil, your mother wishes to speak with you."

"Where's the phone?" Raina asked, unease in her tone.

"She is not on the phone."

Dharr saw the panic begin to form in Raina's face as awareness dawned. "What do you mean she's not on the phone?"

"She is downstairs, waiting for you."

* * *

Raina walked into the elegant private parlor to find her mother standing in the middle of the room, her arms stiff at her sides and her face showing definite signs of disapproval. Regardless of her obvious distress, Carolyn Kahlil still had chic down to a fine art. Her appearance was immaculate, from her blonde bobbed hair to her neat beige pantsuit, even though she'd probably been traveling all night. Raina definitely couldn't say the same for herself. Apparently her mother had noticed since she raked her gaze over Raina's blouse and the gap created by buttons that had been missed in her haste to redress after the earlier interlude.

Raina gave her a quick hug that wasn't exactly returned. "What on earth are you doing here?" she asked, all she could manage around her shock over the surprise visit.

"I booked a flight the minute I received the message you were here." Her mother looked her up and down again, as if she could actually see the effects of Dharr's kiss and touch. "And I should be asking you exactly why you're here, although I could probably accurately guess."

Raina crossed her arms over her middle to cover the gap. "I'm here because Papa needs me. He's been sick. Didn't they tell you that?"

"Yes, they did. But are you sure he's ill?"

Raina did not have the energy to deal with her mother's familiar bitterness. "Yes, I'm sure. And if you don't believe me, go see him."

Carolyn reached behind her and ran one manicured hand over the back of the sofa behind her. "I plan to do that very thing. I definitely want to get to the bottom of this."

"The bottom of what?"

"I'm determined to find out exactly why he summoned you."

Anger began to simmer below the surface of Raina's attempts at a tranquil demeanor. "I've already told you, he's sick. That's the only reason, whether you want to believe it or not. And frankly, I don't care if you don't love him anymore, because I still do."

A flash of pain crossed her mother's face but she quickly recovered. "If you want me to believe your father asked you here only because of his health, then tell me what I've heard about your engagement to Dharr Halim isn't true."

Raina shifted her weight with a nervousness that had yet to subside. "You saw the article in the paper."

Carolyn twisted her watch round and round her slender wrist. "I happened to be heading through the terminal in London to catch another plane and I saw it on a television. I stopped and almost missed my flight."

Oh, great. "It's already made news worldwide?"

"Yes, Raina. Dharr Halim is known beyond Azzril. He's handsome and eligible and royalty. Announcement of his— or should I say *your* engagement—interests a large part of the world. I'm hoping you're going to say this is a misunderstanding, otherwise you'll be making the same mistakes I did."

It was a mistake, but Raina resented her mother's insistence on comparing everyone's life to her own. "Why do you think it would be such a mistake, Mother? You've always been highly critical of my choice in men. If you think about, I could do a whole lot worse than a prince."

"True, if I thought you were doing this because you want to and not because you're bending to your father's will and going ahead with the marriage arrangement. I know how persuasive Idris can be."

"How well I know. He persuaded you into his bed when you were only seventeen."

"Exactly. And we both know what happened after that."

"You made a huge mistake and got pregnant with me."

Carolyn looked wounded. "I've never said you were a mistake."

"Not in so many words, Mother. But at times I believed you resented getting pregnant and now you want to blame Papa, which I think is ridiculous considering it does take two to horizontally tango."

"That's not fair, Raina. I loved your father."

Loved. Past tense. "Fine. But do you really think I'm not smart enough to avoid making the same mistake with Dharr?"

At least Carolyn looked somewhat contrite. "Of course I think you're smarter than that. But I also think that Dharr Halim is as charismatic as your father, and that is very hard to resist."

As if Raina wasn't well aware of that. "I'm not you, Mom. And Dharr's not Papa."

"I'm only concerned about your welfare, Raina. Azzril is no longer your home, or mine. You'll never be accepted here."

You didn't see what I saw a few minutes ago, Raina almost said but decided to hold her tongue. "Look, Mother, you don't have to worry about me screwing up. I'm a grown woman and quite capable of making my own decisions."

"I hope you decide wisely, before it's too late."

Before she fell in love with Dharr, Raina decided. Sometimes she thought it might already be too late. "I need to see Papa now."

Carolyn pushed up her sleeves as if preparing for a fight. "So do I."

"Fine. I'll show you to his room. We can go together."

"No. I want to see him privately first."

"Why?"

"I need to talk to him about a few things."

Raina's concern drove her to grip her mother's shoulders as she gave her a hard look. "Only if you promise me you'll be kind to him. He's not well. He doesn't need any more stress."

"I promise, Raina." Carolyn brushed a kiss across her cheek then stepped back to gather her purse from one chair. "I'll be gracious."

Raina pointed a finger at her. "I'm going to hold you to it. He's on the second floor, third door to the left."

"Thank you, sweetheart. And don't look so worried. Nothing's going to happen. I'm not armed."

As she watched her mother scale the stairs leading to the upper floors, Raina wanted to run after her. At the very least, she wanted to listen outside the door. Instead, she headed toward the place where she'd often gone to find solace in her youth during their frequent visits at the palace. The place where she'd sat with Dharr all those years ago, nursing a huge crush that existed even now. In reality, it had developed into much more than a simple crush.

Regardless, she wasn't going to marry him. They'd both decided that was out of the question. Then why was the prospect so appealing?

Yes, she definitely needed a few moments alone to think, to consider exactly what she was feeling for Dharr and what she intended to do about it. Then she would go see if her mother and father had forgone the fireworks in exchange for a little civility. And that was about as likely as Dharr Halim falling head over heels in love with Raina Kahlil.

Even though she'd insisted on confronting her mother alone, Dharr worried when he sought Raina out an hour later, only to discover that no one seemed to know where she had gone. He had learned that Carolyn had sequestered herself away in Idris's room, without her daughter. Hopefully that would not end badly.

Right now Dharr's only concern was finding Raina. He could think of one place that she might be since he'd been assured she had not left the grounds. He began his search in the gardens behind the palace proper, walking the paths leading to the stone shelter that had provided him with privacy on more than one occasion. Raina's favorite hiding place when she'd been a girl. Several times he'd found her there in the distant past, staring off into space as if she'd had much on her young mind.

He came upon her there today, looking much the same as she had back then, only more mature, and much more troubled. She sat on the stone bench behind the copper wall forming a barrier to prying eyes, heels resting on the edge and her knees clutched tightly to her breasts.

She did not acknowledge him, even when he took a seat beside her. "Did it not go well with your mother?"

Without giving him even a passing glance, she released a sardonic laugh. "Oh, you could say that. Seems news of our engagement has reached across the universe. She saw the announcement on television in London."

Dharr had realized that after learning his father had already been made aware, a fact he would conceal from Raina for now. "You did inform her there is no truth to the rumors."

"Actually, no, I didn't."

"Why?"

She lowered her feet to the ground and shifted to face him. "Because I'm tired of people telling me what to do. On one hand, my father would absolutely love it if I married you. On the other, my mother would rather see me shackled than to have anything to do with royalty. As always, I'm caught in the middle between the two people I love most in the world. And I'm sick of it."

The turmoil in her expression sent Dharr closer to her to take her hands into his. "Where is your mother now?"

"She's still talking to my father privately, and that worries me. I hope she has enough sense to be nice to him. If she does anything to set him back on his recovery, I'll never forgive her."

"Do you honestly believe she will compromise his health?"

"I don't want to believe that but her presence alone might upset him. It's been a whole lot of years since they've been in the same room together."

Dharr acknowledged she needed a sounding board, and he would gladly accommodate her. "You have not recovered from their estrangement."

"No. I wonder if I ever will."

"Have you ever confronted your mother over her decision to leave Azzril?"

"Oh, yeah. Both alone and in front of a few counselors during my rebellious years. But I'm not only angry with her. I'm mad at my father, too."

"It is my understanding your mother left without telling him of her intent."

"Yes, she did. And he just let her go. He never even tried to talk with her after we left. Never tried to get her back. He didn't *fight* for her."

Dharr understood why Idris might not have done that. He knew all too well what it was like to have a woman leave with nothing more than a written missive, taking an integral part of you with her, leaving only an abyss that no one could fill. "Perhaps he believed it would have done no good."

"Maybe not, but he should have tried. If you care about someone, you try until you've exhausted all your options. You don't just let someone you love walk away without at least giving it your best effort. They're both responsible for ruining each other's lives."

"And in some ways, for ruining yours."

She lifted her chin. "No, not my life. I haven't let them do that."

The bravado in her tone sounded false to Dharr and perhaps she was right, but only partially. Her parents may not have ruined her life, but they had dealt her a blow from which she had yet to recover. He could relate to that type of misery.

Even though he wished to stay with her and offer more consolation, he had several tasks he had to complete before days' end. "I must leave. Two days from now, we will be having a reception for a group of European diplomats and I am involved in the planning."

"Really? What country?"

"A very small principality known as Doriana. Perhaps you've heard of it?"

"Yes, but I don't know a thing about it. Geography was never my strong suit."

"It is situated in the Pyrenees near France. The king is a good friend and former Harvard colleague."

Her expression brightened. "Will I get to meet him?"

"He will not be in attendance since his wife has recently given birth. But you will be my special guest at the reception."

She favored him with a smile. "You know that's only going to make matters worse if I show up. Then everyone's going to think we're definitely an item."

He kissed her cheek. "Let them think what they will. I have no cause to hide you away in seclusion."

She gave him a mock pout. "Well, darn. I was hoping we could enjoy a little seclusion after everyone goes to bed tonight. Finish what we almost did in the conference room before my mother came calling."

Dharr would like nothing better, but too much was now at stake. "I'm afraid that would not be wise considering we are all staying on the same floor."

"True, and why is that?"

"The rest of the palace bedrooms are undergoing renovations."

She toyed with the top button on his shirt. "That's too bad. Maybe we could find a nice spot under a drop cloth. Or maybe a corner in the attic."

Dharr began to feel the familiar sexual stirrings and did his best to quell them. "I have work to do."

"And I guess I need to go and make sure there hasn't been any bloodshed between my parents."

Dharr offered his hand, which she took without hesitation. Even though he knew better, he couldn't resist kissing her, long and hard.

Once they parted, Raina smiled again as she kept her arms circled around him. "Thanks for giving me something nice to remember. And thanks for letting me vent."

"My pleasure." And it was, more pleasure than he'd ever thought possible. "I suppose I will see you again tonight during dinner."

"And after dinner?" she asked hopefully.

He touched her cheek, hating what he needed to say, yet knowing it had to be said. "Raina, too many people know, or believe they know, what is going on between us. With your mother now on the premises, it would be best if we discontinue our intimacy."

She lowered her eyes before contacting his gaze again. "You're probably right. But it was nice while it lasted."

More than only nice, as far as Dharr was concerned. "I will never forget what we've shared."

"Neither will I, and if you change your mind, there's something you need to know about my mother. She can be totally oblivious when it comes to what's going on right under her nose."

* * *

"Tell me, Dharr. Exactly what have you been doing with my daughter?"

Raina nearly choked on the bite she'd forced down her throat. For the past two nights, her mother had remained rigid and silent, barely civil to anyone, including Dharr who had joined them. Unfortunately he hadn't joined Raina in her bed. Hadn't sought her out even to give her a quick kiss. And oh how she'd needed him after she'd walked on eggshells with both her parents. Obviously the shells had just been shattered.

When Dharr led off with, "Raina and I—"

"Don't think that's an appropriate question," Raina finished for him.

"I believe it is a very fitting question, my child," her father said. He'd been practically bedridden for days and now he was seated at the end of the table, fully dressed and looking as if he were holding court. Dharr had taken his place at the opposite end, leaving Raina and her mother positioned across from each other to face off, which they definitely were at the moment.

"I can't believe you're actually taking her side, Papa."

"He's not taking sides, Raina," Carolyn said. "He's asking questions, and so am I. We don't understand what's going on between the two of you."

Raina gritted her teeth. "And that's really not any of your concern considering we're both of legal age and free to do as we please."

Her mother's eyes widened. "Are you two sleeping together?"

Not nearly enough, Raina thought. But before she could issue a protest, her father jumped back into the fray. "I would certainly hope that is not the case," he said, his features as hard as the chair beneath Raina's bottom.

Dharr continued to watch the verbal volley and Raina wouldn't blame him a bit if he decided to leave. Right now she could use him as an ally, but she understood why he wouldn't want to dive into the interrogation. Too many thorns in this bed of familial nonbliss.

Raina stiffened her frame and her resolve not to buckle under pressure. "You both can think what you will, but I'm not going to tell you anything other than Dharr and I are friends." Very good friends. "And neither will he."

Her mother dabbed at her mouth with a pristine white cloth napkin, then pursed her lips in displeasure. "Your father and I believe otherwise, Raina. We've discussed this at length. And we have a right to know exactly how far this relationship has gone."

Raina drummed her fork on the table before dropping it with a *plunk* on her plate. "Obviously you've discussed me at *great* lengths without my knowledge. I tried to see Papa twice today only to be told by Badya that I wasn't welcome."

Idris reached to his right and patted Raina's hand. "That is not true, daughter. You are always welcome. Your mother and I simply needed to catch up on several issues."

Raina pulled her hand from the table and wrung the napkin resting in her lap. "And you spent all that time talking about me?"

Carolyn's gaze flitted away. "For the most part."

Her mother appeared to be blushing, something Raina had rarely witnessed. Odd, but then so was this entire gathering.

Her appetite completely gone, Raina tossed the napkin onto the table and posed the question foremost on her mind. "What else did you discuss?" She braced for the bitter word *divorce*.

Carolyn's eyes went wide. "That is none of your business."

"Oh, I see. My parents' conversation about me and Lord only knows what else is none of my business, but mine and Dharr's relationship is yours? Sorry, Mom, but that doesn't cut it anymore. And I'll make you a deal. If you stay out of my business, I'll stay out of yours. Agreed?"

Her papa rubbed his jaw, indicating his increasing discomfort. "Raina, we are only concerned about your welfare. We want to make certain that if the rumors of your engagement are valid, you both have thought over that decision carefully. We would not be pleased if you make a mistake you cannot rectify."

Now that beat everything she'd ever heard to this point in her twenty-five years. Raina raised both hands, palms forward. "Wait a minute. If I'm not mistaken, you're the one responsible for the marriage arrangement, Father dear. And if I recall, you're the one who for years has been telling me what a nice guy Dharr is. How I should really consider following tradition. How he would be my perfect mate. And then that quote in the newspaper. Now you're telling me you've changed your mind?"

"We're just being cautious," her mother said. "We want to make sure you don't rush into anything."

All the years of resentment crowded in on Raina, robbing her of the last remnants of patience. "Well, believe me, I promise that I'm not going to get pregnant, if that's what's worrying you. I also promise that if and when I decide to marry, I'm not going to run out on my husband then spend years living a lonely life in an apartment with only a cat as company. Or holed up in a dusty mansion alone, pretending everything's okay."

Idris slammed his hand down on the table, rattling the dishes and startling Raina out of her tirade. "That is enough, daughter. You should not speak to your parents in that manner, especially your mother."

Raina's mouth dropped open then shut until she finally recaptured her verbal skills and enough sense not to cuss a blue streak. "You're defending her? Have you forgotten she left you in the middle of the night taking your only daughter away from you?"

"Your father understands why that happened," Carolyn said. "We've talked about that."

"Oh, yeah? Would someone like to explain it to me?" Too angry to be reasonable, Raina pushed back from the table. "Never mind. I'm not sure I want to hear it."

"Raina, please sit back down," her mother said.

Idris stood but made no move to stop her. "Your mother and I ask that you visit with us a while longer."

She gripped the chair forcefully as she pushed it beneath the table. "Not tonight. I'm tired and I'm going to bed. But you two feel free to stay up and discuss my life further. Right now I just want to be left alone."

Before leaving the room, she sent Dharr a quick look of apology before leaving him with her parents, practically defenseless. However, she figured he was more than capable considering he was in charge of a whole country. And he would probably need every diplomatic skill he possessed.

Nine

What he'd lacked in diplomacy at dinner, he'd made up for in lies. Not exactly lies, Dharr decided, but an omission of the truth. Yet he'd felt compelled to defend Raina's honor even if he had angered her parents in the process. Even if he had not necessarily honored her.

Now alone in the conference room where he'd met with Raina two days ago, he debated whether to seek her out, or leave her to her solitude as she'd requested. Yet he knew if he did find her, exactly where that would lead—back into his bed. Back into her body. Back into oblivion.

He stood over the museum blueprints laid out on the table, yet he could not focus on anything other than his desire to be with her. To be close to her. To make love with her. Because of his demanding schedule, he'd resisted those urges for forty-eight hours, and his resistance was waning.

When the knock sounded, his irritation increased, until the door opened to the object of his distraction.

Raina entered wearing the same clothes she'd had on at dinner, a tailored pink sleeveless top held together by a zipper and white slacks that formed to the curve of her hips. That zipper had captured his attention all through dinner and he saw no end to his fascination with it, or with her.

"May I talk with you a minute?" she asked.

He straightened and shoved his hands deep into the pockets of his slacks to quell the urge to go to her and without hesitation, touch her everywhere. "Please. I'm afraid I'm making little progress in my work tonight."

She stepped forward to the table opposite him. "I want to apologize for leaving you to confront my family alone."

"I managed."

She brushed her hair from her shoulders. "What did they say to you after I ran out?"

"Basically the same questions they asked of you. The state of our relationship. Whether we had been intimate."

He could see the tension seeping into her face and her frame. "What did you tell them?"

"I told them that they should respect our privacy. We are both adults and what transpires between us is our concern. I also informed them that should we agree to be forthcoming with more information, we would do so if and when we are ready."

Now she looked pleased. "Did my father threaten you after that?"

"No, although I believe he was practicing restraint solely for the benefit of your mother."

"And they bought all that without any protest?"

"I did not give them the opportunity as I took my leave and retired here."

"Thanks for defending me. I hope that doesn't come back to bite you on the butt."

He considered requesting she not reference anatomy in

their conversation. "I will stand firm in my resolve." His resolve was not the only thing standing firm when she strolled around the table and came to his side.

"Is this the museum?" she asked.

Her proximity made it difficult for Dharr to concentrate. But at least they could now discuss a more pleasant subject aside from her parents' grilling. "Yes. What I've been working on for the past two days. These are preliminary blueprints." He indicated the drawings of the various halls. "Exhibits will go here and the foyer will feature sculpture. That leaves a large space to the west. I am still considering its use."

Raina bent and surveyed the plans, holding her long hair back with one hand. "That's easy. You take part of the space and you build classrooms." She pointed a slender finger. "And here, you have a gallery devoted to the local children's art."

"Children?"

She faced him, leaning a hip against the table. "Sure. You'll give them an outlet for their creativity, something to do to keep them off the streets after school. I would've killed for this kind of opportunity when I was younger. That would've saved Badya many a trip into the village looking for me when I'd escaped for a little adventure."

Dharr smiled with remembrance. "I recall you were often seen running through the streets, absent of shoes and covered in dirt, poor Badya chasing after you."

"It sure beat hanging out at the house all day with those boring tutors. A girl has to have a little adventure now and then."

Dharr greatly wanted to give her adventure now, with or without shoes. "This program you're proposing. I assume it would be free to all who participate."

"Of course. Not everyone has your money or means. I'm sure you can find volunteers to teach and a few benefactors to fund the supplies."

"Yes, I could." He came upon a spontaneous idea, one that he doubted she would consider, but at least he could try. "Perhaps you should think about returning here to teach."

She turned her attention back to the blueprints. "I couldn't do that. I already have a job, and it pays. Besides, that would leave my mother all by herself. As mad as she makes me sometimes, she still needs me."

And so do I. The thought vaulted into Dharr's brain so quickly it took him aback. He refused to recognize its validity for to do so would put him in emotional straits. "What about your father?"

"He's managed without us. I suspect he still will. In fact, I wouldn't be a bit surprised to learn he has a mistress somewhere. Maybe several."

"That is not so."

Her gaze snapped to his. "How do you know?"

"Even a man of your father's caliber could not be discreet enough without rumors reaching the palace. He has maintained a reputation beyond reproach. He has had no other women."

"If you say so, but I find it hard to believe he's been celibate for eleven years, if not longer. And I still can't believe he spent all day in a room with my mother and they're not fuming at each other. In fact, they seemed almost amiable at dinner."

"Perhaps they are considering reconciliation."

"My guess is they're finally discussing divorce."

No matter how hard she'd tried to disguise it, Dharr heard the pain in her voice. "I realize that would be very difficult for you."

She turned and leaned against the table then stared at the bookshelves behind him. "You know, I don't really care anymore. As long as they move forward with their lives. This whole limbo thing is ridiculous."

She did care, that much Dharr realized. If only he could think of something to console her. If only he could take her pain away.

Pushing away from the table, she walked to the glass doors where she'd made her first appearance as the prospective wife to the crown prince. "Come here and show me where the museum's going to be."

Dharr walked up behind her, careful not to touch her and in turn, crush his control. He pointed toward the base of the mountain silhouetted against the night sky. "Do you remember Almase?"

"Yes. The rocks shaped like diamonds, not far from the Minhat ruins." She regarded him over one shoulder. "That's a wonderful site. I used to play there as a child. But aren't you afraid you're going to destroy it during construction?"

"We have considered that carefully. The museum will be built adjacent to the formation. We'll use materials that will create the illusion that the structure blends into the mountain."

"That sounds wonderful."

So was she, in many, many ways. "It will be, once it is done. We are hoping to have the museum completed in eighteen months, which is why I need to finalize the plans."

She turned and rested her palms on his shoulders. "Take me there."

As much as he wanted to do that, the following day would be full of meetings and tours with the Doriana diplomats. "I am afraid my schedule will not allow that tomorrow. Perhaps the next day?"

"Tonight. Take me there now."

"It is late, Raina. And too dark to see much."

She slipped her arms around his waist. "Exactly."

"The desert is not always friendly after dark."

"I trust you'll protect me. Besides, Almase has had so

many visitors, I doubt any vipers or scorpions still hang out there." She stood on her tiptoes and gave him a soft kiss. "I'll make it worth your while."

At that moment, he would do anything for her. Anything, except put her in peril. "Your mother and father could be tracking our whereabouts."

"I know and that's why we can't go to our rooms. If they happen to find out we've left, we only have to say we went for a midnight drive. And that's if we care what they think, which I don't. I only care about being with you. It's been two days and it seems like twenty. I've missed you."

He had missed her, as well. Ached for her, in fact. "I am still questioning the wisdom in this plan."

Her smile was sultry, fueling a searing heat deep within Dharr. "Let's do something daring, Dharr Halim. Let's get out of here and leave all our responsibility to family behind. Let's make love in the desert."

He lowered his head and took her mouth, an overture to the pleasure he would surely give her in answer to her fantasy. "You are very difficult to refuse."

"Then don't refuse me."

Dharr left Raina at the bedroom door with a brief kiss and instructions to meet him on the first floor as soon as she'd changed. She made quick work of shrugging on her jeans and pulling on her sneakers. She wasn't quite so fast when she fumbled with the buttons on the oversize oxford shirt. On afterthought, she retrieved the condoms from the drawer where she'd hidden them away, a guarantee he wouldn't have any excuse not to follow through. It took all of ten minutes, tops, before she was sprinting down the stairs on the way to her late-night rendezvous.

She pulled up short when she found Dharr standing at the

bottom landing, wearing his own pair of faded jeans, an equally washed-out crimson Harvard T-shirt pulled tight against his chest and a pair of brown lace up hiking boots. His dark hair was ruffled, probably from his own haste to dress, and he looked as if he'd morphed from premiere prince to college man. The effect was so devastating on Raina's composure that she almost suggested they march back up the stairs to a bedroom so she could peel every article of clothing away from his killer body.

Instead she hopped down the final steps and said, "I'm ready."

"As am I."

Following a quick, chaste kiss, Dharr took her by the elbow and guided her through a labyrinth of hallways until they reached a door that opened to several concrete stairs leading downward. At the bottom, Dharr pounded out a code, opened another heavy door and led her into an underground concrete garage housing several vehicles.

Once there, they came upon two men chatting it up in the corner near the hood of one sedan. When they noticed Dharr, they immediately came to attention in a military stance. Dharr made his request in Arabic for the keys to a Jeep. Amused, Raina watched the men practically falling all over themselves to retrieve them from the safe recessed into the wall.

Dharr told Raina to follow him to a black and beige Jeep parked in the corner among more sedans. He opened the door for her then rounded the hood to position himself behind the wheel. In a matter of moments, they were racing through the garage to the exit where a solid steel gate rose like the entrance to a mystical cave, revealing the magical night.

They maneuvered the lengthy drive at a speed Raina decided was well beyond the limits of safety before Dharr stopped at the guard station to address the sentry, saying little more than they were going for a drive. The man did not look at all pleased when Dharr insisted he did not need an escort, nor did he want one. But at least the guard opened the gate without further argument aside from some under-the-breath mutterings Raina couldn't quite distinguish.

Soon they worked their way through the silent streets of Tomar at a fast clip until Dharr reached the place where pavement turned to dirt. Then he stopped the vehicle, put it in park and turned to Raina.

He reached over and sifted her hair through his fingertips without speaking.

"What are we waiting for?" Raina asked.

"Before the road becomes rough, I wanted to do this."

Cupping her jaw in his palm, he leaned over and kissed her deeply, providing a perfect lead up to what she hoped would come later. He broke the kiss, frowned then following a rough sigh, slapped his palm against the steering wheel. "We have to go back."

He'd changed his mind, exactly what Raina had feared. "Why?"

"I have forgotten something again."

Straightening her legs as far as they would go, she fished through her pocket, pulled out two condoms and dangled them from her fingertips. "Do you mean these?"

His smile formed slowly, seductively. "Then I suppose we are ready."

"You don't know the half of it."

He rested his hand on her thigh. "But I promise I will."

"Good. And before we head out again, can you take the top off?"

He grinned. "You wish me to undress you now?"

Raina laughed, prompted by his show of humor and a lightness of being so welcome after the tumultuous meeting with her family. "That's a thought, but I meant the top on the Jeep."

"Whatever you wish, I will gladly accommodate you." Before she could say more, Dharr slid from the seat and commenced unzipping and folding back the covering, revealing the inky sky. Looking upward, she took in the glorious sight, realizing she'd lived so long in the city, she'd forgotten how brilliant a host of stars could be. How the desert during the day could be unrelenting, but at night it took on a life of its own—mysterious and seductive, like the man whose company she craved.

Dharr returned to the driver's seat, put the Jeep in gear and took off. They scaled the bumpy scrap of road, climbing upward through the mountainous terrain, heading toward a heaven of their own making. Fifteen minutes later, they turned off the main road and stopped at a circular clearing facing the valley below. Dharr left the vehicle while Raina simply stared at the spattering of city lights, knowing that most everyone was preparing for sleep while she was wide awake and wired. The view was breathtaking, but then so was her escort as he held out his hand for her to take.

To Raina, he was an integral part of the panorama—dark, mystifying and somewhat dangerous. Not in the sense that he made her afraid, but he was a huge threat to her heart. He'd already won a good part of it. Tonight he might claim it all.

Guided by the light of the near-full moon, hand in hand they ascended a rock-strewn path, taking them higher into the elevations above Tomar. Although Raina hadn't been to this particular place in over a decade, she had no trouble recognizing the diamond-shaped rocks pointing upward and to her right, the base of the mountain known as Galal—majestic—and very fitting. But it couldn't compare to Dharr Halim, equally magnificent and strong. And all hers tonight.

Giddy could best describe her current mood. And drunk with the freedom of being there with him, alone, knowing that anything she asked of him, he would try to give to her. She planned to return the favor.

"Come with me over here," he told her, his voice low and controlled, toxic to her senses.

She followed him to one steep embankment where he released her then began to climb. At the top, once more he held out his hand to her. "You must see this view."

"What's on the other side?"

"Flat rock that leads to the cliff."

Raina didn't mind heights as long as she was in a protected environment, with the exception of airplanes. But she wasn't feeling too confident about standing on weather-worn stone where one false move could send her over the edge.

When she hesitated, Dharr said, "It is safe. I will not let you fall."

Oh, but she already had—for him.

Clasping his large hand, she allowed him to pull her up. He turned her around to face the valley, his arms wrapped firmly around her and his chin resting atop her head. "This is the place I would come when I wanted to escape. I would view the city laid out before me, knowing it served as a reminder of why I accept my duty without question. I have vowed to see it thrive."

"Azzril is very much a part of you."

"And you, Raina."

She shook her head. "Not anymore. Too many bad memories."

"More than the good?"

She couldn't lay claim to that. "I guess I do have quite a few good."

"Except for your parents' disagreements."

After thinking a moment, she said, "You know, I only heard them fight one time, not long before I left with my mother. Maybe that's why it all came as such a shock. Maybe they just didn't want me to know how miserable they both were, although for the life of me, I can't remember anything but their love for each other. I have no idea what changed, but I guess I'll never know."

He tightened his hold and whispered, "We will make our own memories tonight. Good ones to replace the bad. Beginning now."

Remaining behind her, Dharr began to work the buttons on Raina's shirt until he had the placket completely parted. He held it open, allowing the breeze to flow over her bare breasts, tightening her flesh from the cool draft of air. Yet Dharr warmed her with his palms, playing her gently, thoroughly, until she grew winded with the same helpless need for him.

But then he dropped his arms and left her with only a whispered, "Wait here."

Raina had no intention of going anywhere without him. She sat on the rock opposite the view to watch Dharr as he strode to the Jeep. He pulled out a blanket and came back to her, spreading the multicolored woven throw over the stone surface. Obviously he was more prepared than she'd thought.

She took his offered hand and he drew her up into his arms, against the solid wall of his chest. He held her for a long moment before he stepped back, pushed the blouse completely away from her shoulders then tugged his own shirt over his head. They discarded the rest of their clothing in haste, piling the shirts and jeans onto the blanket to provide more cushion. They embraced again, holding each other closely, exploring with their hands in places they had touched before, yet the intimacy took on a dreamlike quality.

In her mind's eyes, Raina could imagine how they would

appear from below—two lovers silhouetted against the night, insignificant compared to the imposing surroundings, yet important to each other, at least for now. She took the image and mentally filed it away, knowing that some day she would put it on canvas, immortalizing them both captured in this precious moment.

Dharr laid her down gently on the blanket then kissed her much the same—a meaningful kiss that soon turned evocative, exciting. He moved his warm lips to her neck, toying with her hair as he continued his downward journey to her breasts, drawing one nipple deep into his mouth, then the other. Lower he traveled, his lips drifting over her abdomen before coming to rest between her thighs, creating a barrage of thrilling sensations in Raina.

She slid her fingers through his thick hair while he continued to encourage her to completely let go, using his tongue and lips and hands, washing away all uncertainty of her feelings for him. The stars above her fell out of focus and the wind picked up, bringing with it a mélange of scents and sensations. Time seemed to suspend as her body trembled with impending climax until she could do nothing more than give in to its force. She felt weak, boneless, the ground beneath her unforgiving, yet she didn't care. She only cared about him.

Intent on proving exactly how much she cared, after Dharr worked his way up her body with more open mouth kisses, she nudged him onto his back and took the same path down his torso as he had with hers, tracking the trail of dark hair with her lips until she reached her goal. He hissed out a sharp breath when she took him into her mouth. A murmured word of pleasure followed, then her name drifting on the breeze with a reverence that made her heart ache with longing.

She remained unrelenting in her movements, even when he asked her to stop because he could no longer hold on. She didn't stop until he pleaded with her, then told her how greatly he needed to be inside her. Now.

She smiled as she took a condom and sheathed him, and he smiled back when she straddled his hips and guided him inside her. But his smile disappeared as she set the pace, slowly at first then more frantic. Watching his face grow taut, his eyes grow hazy, was magical, and admittedly powerful, knowing that she could take him exactly where he had taken her. He clasped her hips as his body surged up with his own climax, sending Raina remarkably over the edge again. She collapsed against his chest, gasping for air, grasping for a hold on her runaway emotions. She was totally lost when Dharr kissed her again with profound tenderness.

How could she want him so much? How could she be so completely consumed by a man that she honestly didn't care if she ever returned to reality? Or ever returned to California, for that matter.

Despite her need to be cautious, she craved being close to the fire he'd continually created in her. Only stolen moments, she tried to tell herself but quickly banished those thoughts. She would pretend it was forever, even if it was only for to-night.

Dharr Halim had always been pragmatic. Analyzing numbers, not emotions, had been his forte. He had an aptitude for finance, never feelings. He admired art yet he could never imagine putting paint to paper. And creating poetry had not once entered his mind…until now.

With Raina next to him, cast in the first signs of dawn, he felt as if he could quite possibly write a sonnet.

At the moment they were seated on the hood of the Jeep, the blanket their only cover, their arms providing shelter from the morning cold. For hours they had talked, then touched, culminating in more lovemaking as intense as the first. He'd made it his mission to know as much as he could about her, both body and mind. She had done the same. He had never known a more willing lover, and he had never revealed as much of himself to any woman. Yet one part of him she did not know—his heart.

He felt no need to open old injuries only to bleed some more. He chose to cherish this time with her without discussing past mistakes, realizing these moments could be their last.

"I guess we should go now," she said, both her tone and her eyes laden with regret.

"Yes, we should."

"Which means we have to get dressed."

"True."

"Unless we want to drive back to town naked, although I'm not sure that would be good for your image."

If he thought for a moment they could do that without discovery, he certainly would. He would touch her on their return until he had given her more pleasure, just so he could watch her face. "I suppose you are right."

Yet neither of them made a move other than toward each other, their lips uniting again in a kiss that had Dharr reconsidering his need to return to his responsibility.

"Dharr," Raina murmured against his mouth. "We really do need to leave now."

He reluctantly pulled away and groaned. "If we must."

"We must."

They gathered their clothes and dressed on opposite sides of the vehicle at Raina's insistence. A good idea, Dharr decided considering he was on the verge of making love to her again despite his pending duties.

They traveled back to the palace without speaking, their fingers entwined, resting on his thigh. In the garage, they walked past the guards who averted their eyes, as if he and Raina were invisible. Once they reentered the palace, Dharr maintained his distance until they reached the staircase leading to the upper floor. Absent of restraint, he grabbed Raina's hand and turned her into his arms before she could scale the first step.

He kissed her again, stroked her hair, held her close as if he could not have enough of her. Raina proved to have the most presence of mind when she broke the kiss and said, "Someone is going to see us."

He lowered his lips to her throat. "I do not care."

She bracketed his face and forced him to look at her. "You say that now, but you would care if my father happened down the stairs. He's an early riser."

Dharr pressed against her. "And so am I."

"You're incorrigible, too." She backed away from him and climbed the first two stairs without turning around. "I'll see you tonight."

When he started toward her, she pointed a finger. "Stay right there until I get a good head start."

He propped an elbow on the banister and smiled. "And if I do not?"

"Then I won't be responsible when I lose it and tackle you on the landing, tearing off your clothes while shouting 'Take me now,' which will undoubtedly wake the entire household."

With that, she spun and sprinted up the stairs, leaving Dharr to watch her until she disappeared.

He decided to return to his office before retiring to his room to change. If not, he would be tempted to join her in bed for the rest of the day. He had too much to accomplish to be distracted, but as he began to review his schedule, he could not banish the images of Raina—her face flushed with heat when he'd made love to her and again with cold in the morning light. A face he would welcome waking up to each and every morning.

To continue considering such a thing would prove to be unfavorable to his plans. He would not marry in the near future. Not until his father insisted it was time to produce an heir. Only then would he choose a woman who was like him. A woman who possessed a certain amount of independence. Who enjoyed art. Who had a passion for life and a propensity for adventure.

Dharr realized he had just described Raina Kahlil—a woman who would be gone in a matter of days.

After Raina left the shower and crawled beneath the covers to grab a few hours' sleep, someone knocked on the door. Since Badya never came around this time of morning, she suspected she knew who that someone might be.

She grabbed the handle and said, "You are one stubborn guy," only to find her mother, not the sheikh, standing on the other side.

Raina tugged on the hem of her gown and bit her lip almost hard enough to draw blood. "Why are you up so early, Mom?"

"I've been visiting with your father." Without an invitation, Carolyn pushed into the room then spun around. "Where were you last night?"

Oh, joy. "How do you know I wasn't right here?"

"Because I came up to say good-night and you weren't anywhere to be found."

"I went out for a drive."

"With Dharr?"

"Yeah. Sorry I missed my curfew."

Carolyn folded her arms in true disapproving-mother fashion. "What is really going on between the two of you?"

This was so ridiculous, and typical. "Mom, I've already told you, and so has Dharr, that what we might or might not do together is really no one's business but ours."

"I'm worried about you, Raina. I'm worried you're getting in too deep."

Raina had to admit her mother had valid concerns. "I'm mature enough to handle it, Mother."

"You keep telling me that, then you disappear in the middle of the night like some teenager with a man who might as well be a stranger."

"He's not a stranger. I've known him for years."

"Exactly *how* well do you know him now?"

Raina was way too weary to dance around the truth any longer. Hanging onto her last scrap of self-control, she calmly said, "We're lovers, Mother. Are you happy now?"

If she was at all shocked over the revelation, Carolyn hid it well. "Are you going to marry him?"

"That has not even entered my mind." Not more than once or twice.

"But you're in love with him, aren't you?"

"What makes you think that?" So much for trying to keep calm.

"As they say, it's written all over your face."

Raina turned around and began to aimlessly arrange her toiletries on the dresser. "What do *they* know?"

Her mother came up behind her and rested a hand on her shoulder. "I've seen that same look on my own face. You're burning for him."

Burning? Raina stared at her reflection in the mirror. Funny, she didn't look as if she were on fire, even though in Dharr's presence, that couldn't be more true.

She shook off her mother's hand and faced her. "Okay, I admit I do have feelings for him. But it doesn't matter. We agreed from the beginning this thing was only temporary. Neither of us wants a commitment." How incredibly false she sounded.

Her mother's expression turned sympathetic. "Oh, sweet-heart. I'm sorry. I hate seeing your heart breaking."

"My heart is still intact." Even if she couldn't guarantee for how long.

Carolyn braced both hands on her hips. "I ought to give him a good tongue lashing for leading you on. I should tell your father and let him do it."

Alarms rang out in Raina's head. "Do not tell Papa a thing. He doesn't need to know. And you can't blame Dharr for this. We were both in it together."

"But you're the one who fell in love."

Too exhausted to continue, she said, "Mother, I need to sleep some before tonight's reception. Can we discuss this later?" Or never.

She patted Raina's cheek. "Okay. You get some sleep. If you want to talk, come and find me."

When her mother turned toward the door, Raina noticed something very odd about the normally well-groomed Caro-lyn Kahlil. The tag on her slacks was exposed, as were the seams. Her mother's pants were on wrong side out.

"One more thing, Mom."

Carolyn turned, one hand braced on the knob. "What?"

"Were you only visiting with Papa. Or were you *visiting* with Papa?"

Her hand dropped to her side. "I don't understand what you're asking."

Raina gestured toward her mother's slacks. "You're wear-ing the same clothes you had on at dinner last night and best I can recall, you had them on correctly during our meal. Ob-viously you've taken them off at some point."

She looked down, then back up again. "I...uh..."

"You and Papa had a little post-separation coitus?"

"We are still married, Raina."

True, but she didn't even want to think about her own mother and father having sex. No child ever did. Especially a child who'd suffered through their estrangement for years. "Did you even stop to consider his heart condition?"

"He doesn't have a heart condition, Raina. He has a hiatal hernia. He's had it for years. If he doesn't take his medicine, he has chest pains, especially when he insists on eating spicy foods, which he does. His tests were all normal."

Fury caused Raina to grip her hands in tight fists at her sides, her nails biting into her palms. "So this was all a ruse to get me back here. And he got you in the bargain, too."

"That wasn't what he intended. His doctors worried it might be more serious, and he worried he might not ever see you again. So please don't blame him."

Raina was almost rendered speechless. "Mother, you two slay me. For years you wouldn't give each other the time of day. Now you're making whoopee and ganging up on me. What gives?"

She paused for a moment, looking somewhat indecisive. "Sweetheart, your father and I wanted to tell you together, but I guess now is as good a time as any."

"What is it, Mom?" Raina sounded like the little girl again. That same little girl who listened to her mother all those years ago say they wouldn't be coming back to Azzril.

"I'm going to stay here. We've decided to try it again. We've realized we still love each other very much."

How many years had Raina longed to hear that? How many times had she prayed for that very thing? But now, she experienced the sting of resentment and the bite of more abandonment. "That's just great, Mother."

Carolyn looked as if she might cry, something she rarely did. "I thought you would be happy."

Raina traded her guilt over being so harsh for some honesty. "Eleven years ago, I would've been thrilled. Now all I can think about is the nights I stayed awake wanting to go home and wondering why you and Papa split. Have those reasons changed?"

"Honey, I left because I knew how much your father loved his country even after they exiled him for marrying me. I saw him agonizing over it for years. I thought that if I returned to America, he'd try to go back and make amends, which he didn't. There's something else, too."

Raina wasn't sure she had the stamina to hear it, but she might as well get it over with. "What else?"

"After I had you, I couldn't have more children. I wanted to give him a son, an heir, and that wasn't possible. But he told me yesterday he never wanted any of those things, only me. Pride has kept us apart, and love has brought us back together, this time for good."

"That's very poetic, Mother." Raina felt the rise of tears, the joy mixed with the sorrow. She was happy her parents had made amends, but now she would return to California alone. She would also never know that kind of commitment with the man she loved.

Feeling remorseful over her callousness, she hugged her mother and pulled back before she started to sob. "I'm happy for you, Mom. Truly I am. I'm going to miss you, though."

Her mother cupped her cheek. "Your father and I wish you would consider staying. If not permanently, at least for a while."

Stay and face Dharr knowing he would never love her. She couldn't do that. In fact, she didn't want to stay a minute longer, but she had promised Dharr she would be at the reception. She planned to keep that promise. Tomorrow morning she would make plans to leave. "I'll be fine. I have a good job. And now that I know you'll take care of Papa, I need to go home."

Home. Had California ever really been her true home? Not really.

"And you won't stay a few more days?" Carolyn asked.

She didn't want to dash her mother's hope, at least not now. "I'll think about it. But right now I really need some sleep."

"Okay, honey. I'll see you tonight."

Raina escorted her mother out, then tried one more time to go to bed, only to be halted by another knock on the door. If she thought it might be Dharr, she would run. Believing that to be impossible, she dragged her feet all the way to answer the summons.

She was glad she hadn't hurried when she found a strange woman with severe short black hair and overdone makeup standing on the other side of the threshold, a long black bag draped over one arm. "Princess Kahlil, especially selected for you."

Raina took the bag and envelope she offered, thanked her and after the woman left, hooked the hanger over the top of the door. She slit open the envelope and read the message penned in bold script.

A special gift for a special woman. A dress fit for a queen. Wear it for me tonight—Dharr

For a queen? Surely he didn't mean… No, she would not read more into this than it was—a thoughtful gesture from a thoughtful man. An incredible man with incredible taste, she decided as she unzipped the plastic and slid it from the garment. The floor-length sleeveless white satin gown, its high collar accentuated with gold braid, would be deemed simple and elegant, but gorgeous.

Raina held it against her and surveyed it in the mirror. She loved it. Tonight she would wear it for him, and hope that he would be responsible for taking it off. Maybe she *would* stay a couple more days.

But she wouldn't be worth anything if she didn't get some rest. Dark circles didn't go well with white satin.

As she finally settled into bed for a nap, she couldn't prevent the excitement and the glimmer of hope. Maybe tonight would be a turning point in hers and Dharr's relationship. Maybe tonight, when they were alone again, she would find the courage to tell him how she really felt. And maybe, just maybe, he might admit he had feelings for her, too.

Ten

When Raina appeared in the entry to the grand salon, Dharr could not put into words exactly how he felt. Mesmerized by her. Proud of her. Lost to her.

The dress fit her perfectly, as he'd known it would when he'd selected it from those the local boutique owner had brought to him. He'd had no difficulty judging which one would fit; he had memorized every inch of Raina's body both by touch and sight. Her hair was pulled up high, three braids woven with gold ribbon trailing from where it had been bound. She wore more makeup tonight, yet it did not mask her beauty even though he preferred the natural color of her lips. When they were alone again later, he would gladly remove the lipstick and the dress. If they had the opportunity to be alone.

As he visited with the Doriana contingency, he covertly watched Raina, her movements refined as she mingled with the guests on the arm of her father. He wondered what it would be like to have her on his arm, showing the world that she was his. But she would not be his, and he needed to remember that. He would do nothing to threaten her coveted freedom. He would not be left with his emotions in shambles again. He would not watch her walk away with his heart, though he wondered if perhaps she would take a part of it with her despite his determination not to love her.

When she moved closer, he gestured her over. She excused herself from the sultan and came to his side, smiling when he said, "Princess Kahlil, this Mr. Renaldo Chapeline, prime minister of Doriana."

The portly balding man bowed and kissed her hand. "*Enchanté*, Princess."

"It's very nice to meet you, as well, Prime Minister."

Chapeline released her hand and regarded Dharr. "You have made a fine choice for a bride, Sheikh Halim."

Dharr glanced at Raina to find her looking at him expectantly before addressing the prime minister again. "I am afraid that what you may have heard are only rumors. The princess and I do not plan to marry. She will be returning to California soon."

He saw something else in Raina's eyes, something he could not define when she added, "Yes, I'll be returning very soon. Now if you'll excuse me, I believe I see my mother summoning me."

Dharr watched her walk away, perplexed to see that her mother seemed preoccupied with the sultan and not at all interested in Raina's whereabouts, and even more confused when Raina stopped to converse with Raneer on her way to join her parents.

"She is a beauty, Sheikh Halim," Chapeline said, drawing Dharr's attention. "I am sorry to hear she is not the one for you."

Yet she could be the one, Dharr realized in that moment. Or would be were she not intent on returning home. He turned his back, refusing to look at her any longer, refusing to acknowledge the soul-deep pain threatening to surface. Refusing to accept that he would soon have to let her go.

Raina summoned her parents into the foyer and prepared for the fall-out. "I wanted to let you both know I'm leaving tonight."

"Tonight?" Her papa's face reflected unmistakable fury. "Have you totally taken leave of your senses?"

Yes, she had, on more than one occasion with Dharr. But she had full control of mental function at the moment. "I have to get back to work. If I leave now, I'll be recovered from the flight by Tuesday at the latest." Even if she wouldn't be quite recovered from her limited time with Dharr.

"That's silly, Raina," her mother said. "Waiting one more day isn't going to matter all that much. We've barely seen you since I've arrived."

No kidding. "I think that's because you and Papa have spent all your time together, and that's okay."

"This is our fault," Idris said. "We have not afforded you much courtesy because we have focused only on—"

"Getting reacquainted," Carolyn interrupted. "But if you stay, we promise we'll pay more attention to you."

"I'm not a child, Mother. I don't need your undivided attention." She offered an unsteady smile. "You both need to catch-up on all the time you've missed together. And I really am happy you've decided to make your marriage work." Finally, Raina thought, but discarded the bitterness for the sake of her family. She couldn't change what had been, but she could learn to embrace what would be—her parents' happiness—even if her own looked bleak.

Her mother's joy illuminated her expression. "We're so glad you're happy, sweetheart. But I still don't know how you're going to manage to get a flight on such notice. Not to mention you'll have to drive miles to the nearest commercial airport."

"I've taken care of that," Raina said. "Mr. Raneer told me that the king and queen are due to arrive within the hour. He also told me I could use the private plane. All he has to do is arrange for another pilot to take me back to California."

Her papa looked handsome in all his royal finery, but no less unhappy. "Then it appears that is settled and obviously we cannot change your mind."

"No, Papa, you can't. I think this is best for all concerned." Especially for Dharr. He'd been so adamant in telling the prime minister their engagement was only a rumor that it seemed no hope remained for a permanent relationship between them. Oddly that's what she'd wanted all along—nothing permanent. But now she wanted so much more. If she couldn't count on some kind of commitment in the future, then no future could exist between them.

Her mother pinned Raina with a knowing look. "Have you told the sheikh your plans?"

"I'll talk to him before I leave." Something she was definitely dreading.

Her papa said, "Then I am to presume there are no plans for you both to marry?"

As badly as Raina hated destroying her father's wishes, she couldn't give him false hope. "No. No plans. There never were. Dharr and I began as friends, and we'll part as friends." She prayed that would be the case. "I'm sure he'll find someone who will make a good queen." And that thought made Raina both angry and sad.

Ready to get the goodbyes finished, she hugged her mother

first, then her papa. "You both take care. Maybe I'll see you soon. You could have a second honeymoon in California."

Raina hated the sadness in her papa's eyes, hated even more that she'd put it there. "God speed, my *záhra*."

"Take care, sweetheart. Call when you're back in California."

"I will."

Raina turned and rushed up the stairs, holding back her tears until she was safely in her room—Dharr's room. While she swiped furiously at her tearstained face, she meant to pull her clothes from the hangers in the closet but instead found herself staring at his clothes. Slowly she ran her fingers over one tailored jacket, then lifted the sleeve and held it against her damp cheek. How terribly silly she was. How incredibly foolish she'd been. And how very hard she had fallen in love like some fickle female who didn't know what was good for her.

One thing she did know to be true—she was good for Dharr. They were good for each other. But if he didn't love her, if he allowed her to walk out of his life for good, then that couldn't be at all true.

Only one way to find out.

For the next hour, Dharr went through the motions of playing the perfect host, fighting the urge to search Raina out until he could no longer fight. He scanned the room filled with guests yet she was nowhere to be found.

He signaled Raneer and took him to one side. "Have you any word on my parents' arrival?"

"Yes. They should be landing at the airstrip in the next half-hour. They hope to make an appearance before the guests disperse."

"Good. Have you seen the princess?"

"No, your grace. But I have spoken with her."

"I noticed. What was that about?"

"She made a request."

"What request?"

"For use of the plane for her return to America."

Dharr attempted to sound as nonchalant as possible though he highly doubted he'd completely hidden his concern. "Did she say when she will be returning?"

Abid tugged at his collar. "She says she must return immediately. Tonight."

Dharr's concern increased. "Has there been an emergency?"

"None that I am aware of."

"Where is she now?"

"As far as I know, in her quarters, packing."

Dharr pushed his way through the guests, muttering apologies as he went. As he ascended the stairs, a thousand questions hurled through his mind. Why was she leaving now? Was he somehow responsible for her departure? Had she intended to go without telling him goodbye?

He wanted answers. Now.

Without bothering to knock, Dharr barged into the room to find Raina seated on the edge of the bed, arranging her clothes in the bag she'd brought with her.

He raked the kaffiyeh from his head and tossed it onto the corner table. "What are you doing?"

She afforded him only a brief glance before going back to her packing, seemingly unaffected by his anger. "I would think that's obvious. I'm getting ready to leave."

"Why now?"

After zipping the bag with a vengeance, she came to her feet. "I have to go back to work. Besides, I'm not needed here anymore."

If she only knew how much he needed her. If he only had the strength to tell her. "And your father? Are you no longer concerned with his health?"

"It appears that he has a stomach problem, not a heart problem. My mother informed me of that this morning, as well as the fact she intends to stay and work on her marriage." She released a caustic laugh. "Imagine that. After eleven years, they're going to carry on as if nothing happened."

"I would think that would please you."

"In a way it does, in another it makes me angry considering all the time they've wasted. But it really doesn't matter what I think. My mother is staying here to take care of him, and I'm free to return to my life in California."

She desired her freedom, not him, something he'd known all along. Dharr's defenses took hold, surrounding his emotions in protective armor. "Apparently you have made up your mind."

"Yes, I have. And thank you for letting me wear the dress. I've hung it in the closet. And I left the lamp for you, a little something to remember me by."

He would need no reminders. Her memory was already deeply etched in his soul. "You need not return any of it. It is all yours. I have no use for it."

"I appreciate that, but I'm sure you'll find someone else who will wear the dress better than me. A true queen."

That would never be true for Dharr. He would never find anyone who could compare to her. Anyone who would make a better queen. A better lover. A better life partner.

Raina retrieved an envelope from the nightstand then handed it to him. "Here. I wrote down a few things I want you to know. You can read it now if you'd like."

Another letter, a different woman, a repeat of history. "I will read it after you are gone. I must return to my guests."

When he saw the disappointment in her eyes, he almost gave in. "Fine. Suit yourself then."

The shrill of the bedside phone caused Raina to jump and

she snatched it from its cradle. "Yes?" A moment of silence. "Great. I'll be down in a few minutes."

After she hung up, she told him, "Your parents are about to land, so I'm going to catch a ride to the airstrip in the car that's scheduled to pick them up."

"It could be some time before they ready the plane for departure."

"I don't mind waiting. But first, I'm going to say goodbye to Badya, then I'll be going."

"You are not concerned with traveling alone?"

Her smile threatened to break through his self-imposed fortress. "I'm sure it won't be quite as pleasant as my trip here, but I'm not afraid of flying anymore. Thanks to you."

A sudden spear of desperation hurled through Dharr. "Is there nothing I can say to convince you to stay?"

She hesitated for a moment before saying, "Obviously not. But there is something you can do for me. Kiss me goodbye."

He wanted to refuse her, to keep up the façade of indifference. Yet when she moved into his arms, he was lost to her again. He touched his lips to hers, memorizing her taste, the soft heat of her mouth, knowing those memories would haunt him for a long time. For a lifetime.

Raina pulled away first and slipped the bag's strap over her shoulder. "At least you have your room back now."

But he did not have her, and that only fueled his discontent. What a fool he had been. Still, he did not want to leave her with angry words. "I will miss your company."

"And I'll miss your teasing, I think. If you're ever in California, give me a call. I'd love to show you the beaches." She nodded toward the painting over the fireplace. "If you ever feel the need to ditch that masterpiece, think of me, okay?"

He would think of her often. Every day. Every night. "Will you return in the near future?"

"Maybe someday."

And perhaps someday he would be over her, although that did not seem likely. He considered voicing his feelings, considered telling her that he wanted her to stay, not for a few days but permanently. But if he remained silent, at least he would not have to hear that she wanted only her freedom. That she could not accept what he had to offer. That she could not accept him.

He touched her face once more. "Peace be with you, Raina."

"And with you, Dharr Halim."

Then she was out the door, leaving Dharr feeling utterly bereft.

He had no time to ponder what might have been. In a short while, he would need to be downstairs to welcome his parents home. In the meantime, he needed to return to his visitors. Duty took precedence over Raina's sudden departure and the letter still clutched in his hand. He would not read it until much later, when he was once again alone.

Still, he needed a few more moments to regroup, to recover from the blow, then he would return downstairs. Collapsing into the chair near the window, he kept staring at the envelope. Kept wondering what she had said in a letter that she could not say to him in person. They had talked about so many things. He thought she trusted him. He had learned to trust her.

Unable to ignore his need to know, he tore open the envelope, withdrew the paper and began to read.

Dear Dharr,
I've never been all that good at verbally expressing my feelings except through my art, but since I can't really draw you a picture, I decided to write down my thoughts.

My mother and father's decision was only part of the reason why I needed to leave. The other has to do with you. I never intended to feel anything for you. Never intended to make love with you. And I definitely never planned to fall in love with you.

But I do love you, Dharr. I only wish I knew who caused you such pain that you've given up on love. I wish I could be the woman who heals you. If you're reading this and you still let me go, then I know there is no hope for us. As I've said before, if you love someone, you fight with all that you have to keep them close. What better proof of true commitment.

Regardless of what you decide to do with this knowledge, I will still love you anyway, and always. Raina.

Dharr read the letter again, absorbing the words, a profound pain radiating from his pounding heart. She had presented him with the ultimate test, urging him to undertake a battle to win her back. He would walk through the fires of hell to do that very thing.

And he would, beginning now, before she walked onto the plane and out of his life.

Raina stared out the sedan's window, her eyes clouded with tears she tried so hard to keep to herself. After she was alone on the plane, then she would cry all the way to California.

The sun was beginning to set over the mountains, washing the terrain in gold and reminding her of the night before in Dharr's arms. At least she had that memory to see her through until she got over him. That could take years, or a lifetime.

For a minute she'd thought they'd entered some sort of dust storm, then she caught sight of the vehicle pulled alongside of the sedan and heard the blare of a horn. She sat up straight, fearing some highway bandit was trying to commandeer the car—until she recognized the driver.

What was Dharr doing there?

She had no time to question his unexpected appearance before the sedan pulled over and Dharr yanked open her door. "Come with me," he told her as he clasped her hand and tugged her from the seat.

She stood in stunned silence while he tossed her bag into the Jeep and told the driver in Arabic to retrieve his parents and tell them he would be detained indefinitely.

He held open the Jeep's door and said, "Get in."

On wooden legs, Raina complied and settled into the seat while Dharr got back behind the wheel and took off. He turned around in the middle of the road, pausing to allow a shepherd herding his sheep to cross the dirt thoroughfare. Then he was off again, leaving a blanket of dust in his wake.

"Dharr, the airport's the other way."

He kept his gaze trained on the road. "I know."

"Where are you taking me?"

He still refused to look at her. "You will see."

It didn't take too long for Raina to realize exactly where they were going when Dharr navigated the back roads up the mountain. They arrived at Almase in record time, thanks to Dharr's speed-demon driving. She had no idea why they were here but she hoped to find out soon. She wouldn't allow herself to hope for more than that.

Rounding the hood in a rush, Dharr opened her door and led her once more to the place where they had made love. He turned her toward the valley, his arms wrapped around her from behind. "Azzril is a part of you, Raina. You belong here. It is your true home."

"Sometimes I don't feel like I have a home anymore."

He turned her around to face him, his arms resting on her shoulders. "You do have a home here, with me."

Hope niggled at her heart. "With you?"

"Yes. You must stay."

"Why?"

"Because you are also a part of me now, as I am a part of you. We would both regret destroying that bond."

Her hope grew stronger but she wasn't quite ready to believe just yet. "Dharr, I'm not quite sure what you're saying."

He hesitated a moment, looking out over the valley before again turning his soulful eyes on her. "What I speak of now, I will not speak of again. There was a woman long ago, when I was at Harvard."

"Elizabeth?"

"Yes. I was young and she was different from any woman I had known. We were very different. She was also my first real lover. She could not accept my culture, or my responsibility. She wanted nothing more than her freedom. She told me so in letter then left without saying goodbye."

"And I did the same thing."

"No, you said goodbye, and you also said something she never did, that you love me."

"I do love you, but I'm still concerned because it appears you've never gotten over her."

"I suppose I have mourned the loss for ten years, shielding myself from that pain. Now I realize that my loss was only felt so intensely because of my age. That losing her was not so great a loss after all. Yet if I lost you, that would be a loss greater than any I have ever experienced, because I have come to recognize that the love I feel for you is the love felt by a man, not a boy, for a remarkable woman. I realize now I was simply waiting for you."

Raina swallowed a gasp. "You love me? Are you sure?"

He gently held her face in his strong hands, forcing her to look into his eyes. "In my life, there have been very few things of which I have been so certain. If you desire it, I will toss away my duty and position. I will give everything up for you. I will follow you wherever you wish me to go, as long as I am with you."

Although shadows played across his features, she could still see the sincerity in his dark eyes, and the love she had been searching for. "You don't have to give up anything, and neither do I. You're right, Azzril is my home. And as they say, home is where the heart is, and mine's definitely with you." This time "they" were absolutely right.

"Then you will stay?"

She slipped her arms around his waist and smiled. "Yes. Does this mean I'm going to be a kept woman?"

"I hope you will be my wife."

Her laugh sounded broken and shaky from another on-slaught of tears trying to make their presence known. "You mean adhere to that silly marriage contract. Where do I sign?"

His own smile faded into a frown as he thumbed one rogue drop from her cheek. "You need not sign anything beyond an official document proving our marriage. What will bind us is our love for each other and nothing more."

"I'm all for that. Does the offer still stand for me to teach art?"

"No."

Raina saw the first real problem in their relationship. "I've worked most of my life, Dharr. I don't intend to sit at the palace and plan social events twenty-four seven."

"Nor do I want that from you. I do want you to be the director in charge of the children's program at the museum. If you still wish to teach, that will be up to you."

She held him close, buried her face against his shoulder, let the tears fall. Unrestrained tears of joy, of love without bounds. He kissed those tears away, then kissed her lips with an aching tenderness. When they finally parted, he sent her another smile. "You will be a revered queen."

Standing on her tiptoes, she kissed his forehead, his cheeks, then his mouth. "Right now I want to be your revered lover, but I guess we really don't have time since you need to get back to your guests. And I need to break the news to my parents that I'm staying for good."

He began to release the buttons on her blouse. "We shall be fashionably late."

Raina returned the favor by working Dharr's buttons, as well. "What are our parents going to think?"

"Our fathers will be grateful, for when we return tonight, I will be escorting my future bride."

Raina had made a beautiful bride. Even though several hours had passed since the wedding, Dharr was still remembering the vision of her walking down the aisle on her father's arm. And following their vows, she had been on his arm, showing the world she was his.

At the moment, Dharr stood in the bedroom he now shared with his new wife, admiring the painting hanging over the fireplace—a man and a woman silhouetted against the desert night, the lights of the city providing the backdrop—replacing the nude he had sold to donate money for the children's program. Raina had completed the masterpiece in less than a months' time while deep into plans for the wedding. And Dharr had missed winning the wager by one week, though he did not care. As far as he was concerned, all three Harvard colleagues had won.

The celebration continued outside the palace, yet Dharr and Raina had excused themselves early. For the past hour, they had made up for time lost together due to their commitments, and their mothers' determination to keep them apart until the wedding. However, they had managed to sneak away a few times in the middle of the night, returning to their favorite place to explore…each other.

"Are you coming back to bed now? I really need a good naked man to warm me up."

Dharr turned to find Raina stretched out on the bed in a provocative pose, nude, a vision not easy to ignore. Yet when he glanced at the clock, he realized he would have to disregard his own need to return to her, at least for a while. "As much as I hate the thought of not coming back to bed, we are scheduled to make an appearance on the veranda in ten minutes."

Her golden gaze raked over his equally nude body. "I dare you to go out there like that."

When he started toward the glass doors, she bolted from the bed. "Dharr, I'm not serious."

He turned and laughed. "Some day you will learn not to dare me unless you expect me to follow through."

She grabbed for her dress laid out on the chair at the bedside and her underclothes from the floor where he had left them. "I'll keep that in mind."

Dharr put on his tuxedo and robes then the kaffiyeh while he watched her dress. He would take great pleasure in removing her clothing again, once he had performed his duty—introducing the future queen to the adoring subjects.

After they were presentable, he took her hand and led her to the entry to the balcony, but before they could proceed, she pulled him to a stop. "Are we going to have to do this every night?"

He grinned. "I certainly hope so. Several times if you are willing."

She frowned. "I meant make an appearance."

"Only tonight. And when we have our first child."

After adjusting his collar, she patted his chest. "You know, my father mentioned that tonight. He wants to know when we're going to give him that grandson, and I told him not to push his luck."

"I prefer not to share you for at least a year, maybe two."

She winked. "I won't argue with that. I'd like to keep you in bed for at least that long."

"And you will have no argument from me." Leaving one arm around her, Dharr gestured toward the doors. "Shall we address the masses now, Princess Halim, so we might return to bed soon?"

"Why of course, Sheikh Halim. The sooner, the better."

"Masses" proved to be an accurate assessment, Dharr realized when they stepped to the railing surrounding the veranda. Two guards emerged from the darkness and flanked them on both sides as the crowd began to cheer. He positioned Raina in front of him, his arms circled around her. She rested one palm on his joined hands and waved with the other while myriad cameras began to flash.

"Great. Now I'm blind," she murmured.

He leaned close to ear. "When we go back inside, we need only to be able to feel our way over each other's bodies."

"And hopefully we won't have some reporter climbing up the trellis to capture that on film."

"I fear we will always have a certain amount of media attention. It is all a part of the life."

"I know. I read the Los Angeles paper today. The article said, 'California Girl Catches A Sheikh.'" She looked back at him. "Do you feel like you've been caught?"

"I feel I have been blessed."

Without regard for their audience or the guards standing close by, without any prompting, he kissed her soundly, thoroughly, bringing about another resounding ovation.

Once they parted, Raina smiled. "You are so good at that."

"Are you prepared to go back inside for more?"

"You don't have to ask me twice."

After a final wave to their subjects, they returned to the room yet remained in each other's embrace.

"Now when are you going to take me on that honeymoon?" Raina asked as she tugged the kaffiyeh from his head and slid the robes from his shoulders.

He reached behind her to lower the zipper on the dress. "Do you still wish to go to California?"

"Yes. I want to show you the beach. Up close and personal." She released the buttons on his shirt. "Without clothes."

"Would you mind if we make another stop while we're in the States?"

"Where?"

"I am scheduled to meet with my Harvard roommates for our tenth reunion in the state of Oklahoma."

She smiled. "So you can all bemoan your loss over that ridiculous wager?"

"So we can celebrate the fact that we have gained much more than we have lost."

Her eyes misted. "If you keep saying things like that, I'm going to cry again. I almost ruined my wedding dress during the ceremony."

"I will remedy that now." He tugged the fabric from her shoulders, allowing the dress to fall in a pool of lace at her feet. "And I will kiss away your tears, but I will never stop proclaiming my love for you."

"I'm going to hold you to that."

"And I am going to hold you, all night. Every night."

She pulled him toward the bed. "What are we waiting for?"

In a rush, they divested each other of all their remaining clothes and he took her back down on the bed. Dharr chose to simply hold Raina for a time, savoring the feel of her body against his, knowing he would never tire of having her in his arms, or his life. They made love again, slowly at first, then gave in to the passion that had consumed them from the beginning.

In the aftermath, Raina rested her head on his chest, her long hair flowing over him like a silken veil. She was nothing like he remembered all those years before, yet she was better, an extraordinary woman in every sense, and she would always be his, as he would always be hers.

Epilogue

In the smoky confines of Sadler's Bar and Grill, three men of status gathered with their wives—the cowboy, the king and the prince—conducting a journey back into their pasts and freely discussing the prospects of their future. Rowdy revelry filtered into the private room, yet no photographers lurked in the shadows, no paparazzi waited to catch a candid photo. Nothing disturbed the camaraderie shared by longtime friends as they passed the hours in the obscure Oklahoma town.

With his arm draped over Raina's shoulder, Dharr watched with amusement as Marc DeLoria teased his wife, Kate, who was still on the phone speaking with their nanny tending their daughters back at Mitch Warner's ranch. Mitch's wife, Victoria, rested one arm across her belly swollen with child—two children, to be precise. Both girls.

Mitch took his wife's hand and asked, "Are you okay, babe?"

She shifted in her seat and grimaced. "I will be if these babies cooperate and make an on-time appearance."

"Which reminds me, Halim," Marc said. "When are you and Raina planning to have a baby?"

Kate snapped the phone closed and elbowed her husband, causing him to wince and drawing laughter from the women. "That's really none of your business, sweetheart."

"Yeah, it is," Mitch chimed in. "We already have a head start with fatherhood, so I think it's time Dharr takes the plunge."

He glanced at Raina then smiled. "We do not plan to have children for a year or two. We do plan to have quite a bit of practice."

This time Raina elbowed Dharr. "You are so bad."

"They're all bad boys," Tori said.

"But that can be *so good*," Kate added with a smile.

Mitch lifted his cowboy hat, ran a hand through his hair and set the hat back into place. "You beat all I ever seen, Dharr. You were the first to be officially engaged—"

"Betrothed," Dharr corrected.

"Whatever," Mitch said. "And you were the last one to marry. You're supposed to produce an heir, and now you're telling us you're not even planning to have a kid for two years?"

"That is correct." He tightened his hold around Raina's shoulders. "And when we do have our first child, no doubt it will be a son."

Mitch held out his hand. "Wanna bet?"

"A banner idea," Marc added. "I propose we wager that the first man to have a son—"

"Hold it right there, Marc," Kate said. "Knowing all of you, that means we'll end up with at least ten kids a piece if none of you are successful."

Mitch turned to his wife. "That's the point. The pleasure is all in the participation. Right, Tori?"

Tori gave her husband a smile, a cynical one. "I don't think now is the time to discuss having a son, honey."

Seeing an opportunity for diplomacy, Dharr lifted his cup of wine. "To our future children and to our wives, who have effectively brought us to our knees and thankfully ruined our wager."

Tori lifted her glass of soda. "I think we'll all drink to that, right girls?"

Both Kate and Raina readily agreed, holding their glasses high.

Marc raised his beer for the toast. "Here, here."

Mitch did the same. "To friendship, the future and three real fine women."

As the party continued with more tall-tales and stories of exaggerated acclaim, all three men conceded one thing. When it came to a remarkable woman, and falling in love, all bets were definitely off.

* * * * *

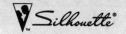

Coming in November 2004

Alexandra Sellers

Powerful sheikhs born to rule and destined
to find their princess brides...

SONS
OF THE
DESERT

SHEIKH'S CASTAWAY

Silhouette Desire #1618

After learning she's a long-lost member of the royal
Bagestani family, Princess Noor finds herself agreeing
to—and then fleeing—an arranged marriage to Sheikh
Bari al Khalid. Sheikh Bari's search for his missing bride
lands them stranded together on a deserted island,
where true feelings are sparked...and real passion
ignites!

Available at your favorite retail outlet.

If you enjoyed what you just read,
then we've got an offer you can't resist!

Take 2 bestselling love stories FREE!

Plus get a FREE surprise gift!

Clip this page and mail it to Silhouette Reader Service™

IN U.S.A.	**IN CANADA**
3010 Walden Ave.	P.O. Box 609
P.O. Box 1867	Fort Erie, Ontario
Buffalo, N.Y. 14240-1867	L2A 5X3

YES! Please send me 2 free Silhouette Desire® novels and my free surprise gift. After receiving them, if I don't wish to receive anymore, I can return the shipping statement marked cancel. If I don't cancel, I will receive 6 brand-new novels every month, before they're available in stores! In the U.S.A., bill me at the bargain price of $3.80 plus 25¢ shipping and handling per book and applicable sales tax, if any*. In Canada, bill me at the bargain price of $4.47 plus 25¢ shipping and handling per book and applicable taxes**. That's the complete price and a savings of at least 10% off the cover prices—what a great deal! I understand that accepting the 2 free books and gift places me under no obligation ever to buy any books. I can always return a shipment and cancel at any time. Even if I never buy another book from Silhouette, the 2 free books and gift are mine to keep forever.

225 SDN DZ9F
326 SDN DZ9G

Name	(PLEASE PRINT)	
Address	Apt.#	
City	State/Prov.	Zip/Postal Code

Not valid to current Silhouette Desire® subscribers.

Want to try two free books from another series?
Call 1-800-873-8635 or visit www.morefreebooks.com.

* Terms and prices subject to change without notice. Sales tax applicable in N.Y.
** Canadian residents will be charged applicable provincial taxes and GST.
   All orders subject to approval. Offer limited to one per household.
   ® are registered trademarks owned and used by the trademark owner and or its licensee.

DES04R   ©2004 Harlequin Enterprises Limited

DYNASTIES: THE DANFORTHS

A family of prominence...
tested by scandal, sustained by passion.

TERMS OF SURRENDER

(Silhouette Desire #1615, available November 2004)

by Shirley Rogers

When Victoria and rebellious David Taylor
were forced into close quarters, former feuds turned
into fiery passion. But unbeknownst to all, Victoria was
no farmhand—she was the long-lost Danforth heiress!
Could such a discovery put an end to
their plantation paradise?

Available at your favorite retail outlet.

COMING NEXT MONTH

#1615 TERMS OF SURRENDER—Shirley Rogers
Dynasties: The Danforths
When Victoria Danforth and rebellious David Taylor were forced into close
quarters on the Taylor plantation, former feuds turned into fiery passion.
But unbeknownst to all, Victoria was no farmhand—she was the long-lost
Danforth heiress! Could such a discovery put an end to their plantation
paradise?

#1616 SINS OF A TANNER—Peggy Moreland
The Tanners of Texas
Melissa Jacobs dreaded asking her ex-lover Whit Taylor for help, but
when the smashingly sexy rancher came to her aid, hours spent at her
home turned into hours of intimacy. Yet Melissa was hiding a *sinful*
secret that could either tear them apart, or bring them together forever.

#1617 FOR SERVICES RENDERED—Anne Marie Winston
Mantalk
When former U.S. Navy SEAL Sam Deering started his own personal
protection company, the beautiful Delilah Smith was his first hire. Business
relations turned private when Sam offered to change her virgin status.
Could the services he rendered turn into more than just a short-term deal?

#1618 SHEIKH'S CASTAWAY—Alexandra Sellers
Sons of the Desert
Princess Noor Ashkani called off her wedding with Sheikh
Bari al Khalid when she discovered that his marriage motives did
not include the hot passion she so desired. Then a plane crash landed
them in the center of an island paradise, turning his faux proposal
into unbridled yearning…but would their castaway conditions lead
to everlasting love?

#1619 BETWEEN STRANGERS—Linda Conrad
Lance White-Eagle was on his way to propose to another woman when he
came across Marcy Griffin stranded on the side of the road. Circumstances
forced them together during a horrible blizzard, and white-hot attraction
kept their temperatures high. Could what began as an encounter between
strangers turn into something so much more?

#1620 PRINCIPLES AND PLEASURES—Margaret Allison
CEO Meredith Cartwright had to keep playboy Josh Adams away from
her soon-to-be-married sister. And what better way to do so than to throw
herself directly into his path…and his bed. But Josh had an agenda of his
own—and a deep desire to teach Meredith a lesson in principles…and
pleasures!

SDCNM1004